TREMBLING EARTH

For my nieces and nephews:
Jon, Ashlyn, Ryan, Nick, and Julia.

TREMBLING EARTH

EARTH

KIM L. SIEGELSON

Philomel Books • *New York*

Patricia Lee Gauch, editor

Published simultaneously in Canada.
Printed in the United States of America.
Designed by Semadar Megged. Text set in 11-point Berling.
Library of Congress Cataloging-in-Publication Data
Siegelson, Kim L.
Trembling earth / Kim L. Siegelson. p. cm.
Summary: In 1864, two boys, one a slave running toward freedom and one hoping to collect the reward for capturing him, make their way through Georgia's Okefenokee Swamp, relying on knowledge the white boy's father, disabled by the war, had passed on to him in happier times.
[1. Fugitive slaves—Fiction. 2. Slavery—Fiction. 3. Fathers and sons—Fiction. 4. African Americans—Fiction. 5. Okefenokee Swamp (Ga. and Fla.)—History—19th century—Fiction. 6. Georgia—History—Civil War, 1861–1865—Fiction.] I. Title. PZ7.S56667Tr 2004 [Fic]—dc22
2003023591
ISBN 0-399-24021-7
10 9 8 7 6 5 4 3 2 1
First Impression

TREMBLING EARTH

"In Dixie Land, I'll take my stand,
To live and die in Dixie."

From the song "Dixie"
by Daniel D. Emmett,
a Northern abolitionist (1859)

Chapter 1

The cloud-softened light of early mornglowm lay atop the swamp water like a slick of pure gold. Hamp stood in the stern of his punt boat, letting his pole drag the bottom until he stalled in the gold-tinted channel that led home to Pinder Island.

"Gilded fine as any street in heaven," Pap had said once of such a spectacle—back when Pap knew more about heaven than he did about hell.

Three long-legged preacher birds lifted their heads up from the floating bonnet lilies they'd been stalking and eyed Hamp, unblinking. He floated for a moment, keeping himself still as a stump, until the birds lost interest in him and went back to gigging minnows. Pap'd taught him how to be quiet and watchful in the swamp, how to make his heart beat with the rhythm of the swamp, to pull it in with every breath so that it flowed through like water flowed through a fish's gills.

"You're a true Cravey swamper, son, born filled of swamp water instead of blood," he'd said once—summer 1861, the day they'd finished building the hunting camp on Rooter Island, just a few weeks before Pap joined up to fight with the Confederates.

Three years and a whole nother lifetime ago, seemed like.

Of all his memories of Pap, he favored that one most; dug it up time and again to gnaw on it, the way a hungry hound slavers over a dry bone for the hint of goodness left in the marrow.

Nothing but silence flowed through Pap now, and nothing filled him up. He was murky and lifeless as a slough ever since he'd come home from the war in the outlands. All the country outside the Okefenokee was outlands, north and south alike. Swampers didn't mix with any outlanders except to sell hides, and what outlanders got mixed up in never mattered to swampers. Until now.

Hamp took aim at a lily pad and spat. Four years of warring was a good part of the twelve he'd been alive, and the reason for it still addled him. Pap called it a revolution, and likened it to the war for independence that'd founded the country. Only this time it wasn't the king of England they were battling, but the elected men up in Washington, mainly Northern Yankees, who didn't want the South to break off from the Union. He said 'twas a law-given right of the people of every state to vote about such things as that, and slave owning.

"We'll not take no more arm twisting," Pap thundered. "Them Yankees think they sit on velvet thrones and everybody's got to bow to 'em. Hain't so! Every man has the God-given right to protect his freedom and his homeland from tyrants and bullies. Comes a time when the only way to keep liberty is to fight for it."

Well, the fighting cost Pap half a leg in the battle at Shiloh Church in Tennessee—a stiff price. Terrible stiff. And the Yanks were still swarming down thick as wasps on a honey pot, determined as ever to make the South bow down. Wouldn't be happy till they'd put it in ruins— charred it as black as their souls, black as the darkies they wanted to set free.

"Dagged bluecoats!" Hamp spit the words out like bitter seeds. "Best stay out of this swamp. One sets a foot near Pinder Island and I'll blast it off for his trouble. I'll drink every drop of blood he sheds and let the gators eat what's left."

The startled preacher birds clapped the air as they took to wing, their necks held forward at an odd, broken-looking angle. In the channel a jackfish leapt up and spoiled the gold-lit path with dark ripples. Hamp rested the pole in the crook of his arm, cupped his hands round his mouth and hallooed loud and long with a hot fury that emptied his chest and scorched his throat.

Two dogs bawled in the distance: Bone and Rascal. And a moment later Ma hallooed her signal that she'd heard him. Hamp planted the pole against the swamp bottom, leaned into it and walked his hands up its length until the boat slid again over the water toward home.

As he passed into the cypress head at the front edge of the island, bay magnolias and hurrah bushes ranked up around him like a green wall. A little yellow-britches scolded *swee-swee-swee*, and a redbird darted into a tangle of vine like a heart caught by a net. A small breeze stirred the moss that draped the cypress tops like tattered, gray rags. Confederate gray.

Brush and cypress knees soon crowded in and narrowed the run to the width of the boat. Hamp laid aside the pole and pulled himself along, using the knees and low-hanging branches as handholds. A black snake dropped from a limb into the water as he passed beneath its sunning spot.

Steadily he forged along, never tricked by the unmarked trail that curved, and then curved again like the snake that'd shimmied off through water dark as strong coffee in the shaded run.

Hamp veered into a tunnel-like opening in the brush no different than twenty he'd passed. It changed quickly from tunnel to a wider channel and then to the open lagoon of Pinder Lake, a deep mirror of water that captured the sky with its scudding clouds. Kneeling, he took up a paddle and stroked toward the landing. The punt glided over the reflection, a swift gray bird with wings tucked.

His younger sister, Neeta, waited for him on the landing, her hair shining nearly as gold as the sunlit water of the channel. As he drew near, she rose to her feet and caught the bow of the punt, held it steady while he gathered up his fixaments: the cane fishing pole and bait tin and wire hooks. When he lifted the string of twelve spotted warmouth perch he'd caught, she grimaced. "We've eat fish nearly every single day this week, and last week, too! We'll all wake up one day with fins for arms. . . ."

Hamp turned on her and gave her a withering glare. He shoved the string of fish at her with such meanness that they slapped against her legs and put slime on her skirt front. "Daggit, Neeta, if you can feed this family better, then do it!" he snapped. "Otherwise tote these up to Ma and keep your grumbling to yourself."

Her chin quivered, but she matched his powerful glare with her own flinty gray eyes. Without a word she yanked the fish from his hand and stomped away through the raw soil of the cornfield a-bristle with tender green shoots.

With a mighty pull Hamp brought the punt to rest on the landing and then dropped down beside it with the idea of letting Neeta gain some distance. He didn't want to eat fish any more than she did. He wished for ham biscuits and cracklin' bread and pork stew. He wished the hogbear hadn't ever found Pinder Island. To his mind, the night it killed their best breed sow marked the beginning of all the bad days since.

The bear struck near middle night on the moon's wane, dark out as pine pitch, or bear fur. He'd not wanted to shoot at it blind for fear of hitting a cow or the dogs or another hog. Ma'd not let him make chase alone, and Pap couldn't.

With bruised hearts they'd stayed inside, helpless to do anything but listen to the poor hog cry. A lonesomer sound he'd never heard of a gloomy night than a hog being slapped and drove off into the swamp, squealing and begging the bear all the while for its life. But seemed like it hurt Pap the worst. He trembled and keened so, covered his ears with his hands, moaned like a haunt in a boneyard.

Even after the hog quieted, Pap acted thataway all the rest of the night. That spooked Hamp more than any-thing. For on that night he'd understood—Pap'd lost more than his leg in the battle at Shiloh, a thing that might not heal. And he'd carried something of Shiloh home with him: a hard, sharp souvenir like a needling sandbur lodged deep in his skin.

Other troubles came, too. After the bear they'd put by a single hog in the smokehouse to last the year, needing the last three as breeders. Ma was down to her last slab of cured bacon. She misered it; used one bitty sliver at a time to flavor the dry cornfield peas from last year's garden.

Plentiful fresh meat could be found in the swamp: deer, raccoon, squirrel, possum, gator, duck, turtle. Hamp did fair at catching the littler critters with traps, middling fair with a slingshot, poor with a bow. Pap said what little they had left of lead slugs and black powder should be saved to protect the hogs and cows from thieving bears, and Pinder from murderous Yankees. Powder and slugs

Kim L. Siegelson

was scarce as hen's lips and selling in the outlands for a king's treasure, the soldiers needing every bit to hold back the Yanks. But without using the gun, it was hard to get hides, and without hides to sell, no way to get what the swamp didn't give: more slugs and black powder, salt for cooking and curing meat, leavening, tools.

And they'd not grown a field of cotton last year, favoring food crops. Who could have figured store-bought cloth and thread would get so costly?

"Twelve dollars a yard for calico, and ten for the cheapest butternut," Ma said. "You'd think it was spun gold! And only ten dollars Confederate money left from Pap's army pay. Well, sir, a yard of cloth might make a fine baby diaper, but not a dress or a shirt or britches."

Hamp's new was Pap's old castoffs, tucked at the waist, patched at the knees and rolled up short in the legs. Neeta's one dress had been mended till it looked like scraps cobbled together, and when she moved, the seams threatened to bust wide open.

They'd never been rich by outlander measures, but Hamp'd never felt poor like he did now. Or so hopeless to fix things. He sighed and hunched his shoulders against the heaviness of an idea he'd had more than once of late: he should leave the swamp and find work in the outlands, maybe trump up his age and sign on as a soldier, or hire on at some dusty outlander farm.

Most farms were being kept by women and girls and boys too young to go warring. At least he'd been there to help Ma while Pap was gone. Every day they'd waited and prayed for him to come home. All that hard work to make sure things didn't fall to ruin, so Pap had a home to come back to, a place to start over.

And then he had . . .

Slowly the sun slipped free of the dark tree line of Pinder Lake's eastern shore and dangled over the water like a ripe persimmon. Hamp stood and tried to shake the gloom away. He gave the punt a final yank, then followed Neeta's footprints up through the field toward home.

C h a p t e r   2

Rascal and Bone met Hamp at the edge of the dirt yard, shimmying their hindquarters and beating the air with their tails. "At least you two is glad to see me," he said, bending to pat them each between the shoulders.

Rascal was Pap's favorite, a purebred bluetick hound with a good nose for tracking, swift legs and a pelt of short white hair that looked like it'd been spattered by wet ash. But Hamp loved good ol' bandy-legged, mud-brown, mixed-blood Bone the best.

Pap had taught him and Bone trapping and hunting at the same time. Bone learned his part of hunting the fastest, but Hamp didn't hold it against him. Fact was, he'd been glad Bone caught on so quick. After Pap left, Bone made hunting without him some easier. Bone helped keep worry from chewing a hole in his belly. Worry that they'd end up eating the laying hens and the milking cow and every last pig in the pen before Pap got home. Worry that Pap wouldn't come home.

"You don't care if it's fish I bring home for two weeks, do you?" Hamp cooed at the dogs. Bone danced along beside him, blocky muzzle split by a lopsided dog grin and floppy purple tongue. He made Hamp want to dance, too, and that's what made Bone the true-blue best. Not one for dancing, Rascal sniffed at Hamp's ankles and, satisfied by the smell of them, trotted off to his shady spot underneath the porch.

Ma came to the door with baby L.B. astraddle her hipbone and chewing on his fingers. "Finest mess of fish you've caught yet," she said, wiping dampness from her forehead with a corner of her apron. "We'll have 'em for supper. Hen eggs and grits is on the table if you're hungry."

"Yes'm," he answered, and doodled his finger under L.B.'s slick chin until he shrieked and flapped his hands.

Neeta and Pap were to the table already. Neeta stopped shoveling food into her mouth long enough to poke her lip out and glower at Hamp as he spooned a mound of eggs into a puddle of grits and took his seat on the bench across from her. Pap didn't speak or look away from whatever held his gaze outside the window. He hadn't touched his plate—sat quiet as a scarecrow, hardly blinking, still but for the one hand that rubbed the stub end of his thigh. Said his foot itched all the time where there wasn't a foot anymore, so he rubbed at the stump and imagined it to be his foot.

Ma walked by and brushed her lips against Pap's forehead. "Did you tell Hamp about Scrub Mooney coming by earlier?"

Hamp scowled and clenched his hands. Scrub was their closest neighbor, and he knew better than to say what he thought. But just hearing Scrub's name pickled him sour. Scrub was outlander by birth, never married, so he brought his laundry and mending to Ma when it needed doing. Always it smelled of boiled turnips and ripe feet. He had the blunt, wrinkled face of an ancient bat, and the same leather-stretched-over-bone leanness about him. He spewed tobacco juice when he talked. And he admitted bold-faced to having not a speck of religion besides hunting and trapping. Ma prayed for him regularly and treated him with extra kindliness in hopes of swaying him to God, but so far he'd vexed her.

"He bring any news about the war?" Hamp asked. "Or just dirty britches?"

Pap licked the dryness from his lips and shook his head. As if a head shake were answer enough, he scooped some egg with the tip of his fork and pushed it into his mouth. He kept his head bowed over his plate like he was saying grace, chewing slowly.

"I went to the landing to tell you, but you jowered at me so fierce and shoved them fish at me," Neeta said.

Beneath the table, she kicked her toes hard against his shin. "Scrub trapped some runaway Negras! Says their owners'll pay a lot of bounty money to get 'em back."

"How much?" Hamp wondered, suddenly interested.

Pap shoved his plate to the middle of the table, most of his food left uneaten. He braced himself for a moment, his neck bent down like he might have been searching for something on the floor between his feet. The image of a cattail stalk beaten over by heavy rain popped into Hamp's mind.

"In the outlands I seen posters offering fifty, a hundred apiece," Pap said. He shook his head. "Damn cotton planters don't mind paying a high price to keep their darkies a-slaving. 'At's all I'll say."

Ma put her hand on his arm and squeezed, her signal that he wasn't to swear. "I'd as soon Scrub let the poor wretches go, and I told him so," she said. "Whoever owned them Negras mustn't have treated them well or they'd not have run off. No telling what torment he'll send them back to."

A hundred dollars for a Negra! Hamp shoved his half-full plate toward Pap's. It galled him. How did the Craveys always come up with the small end of the horn, while other folks got the fat end? Folks like Scrub, who'd never been a master hand at tracking, no matter how he bragged on himself. A dagged outlander who didn't even have religion, for pity's sake.

A hundred dollars . . . A half season of trapping brought less money. Daggit! That kind of money in their coin box would sure ease his worries about leaving the swamp.

"I'll be finished with the wash by afternoon," Ma said. "I told Scrub I'd send you over with his, Hamp. And don't you let him give you one penny for it or you'll march right back to return it, same as last time."

Seemed like Scrub could afford a few coins if he was getting a hundred apiece for darkies. Hamp scrambled for an excuse. "Ma, I was wanting to take Bone out to Duck Pond Lake. Check my traps on Rooter Island. Scrub's place is east, slap in the wrong direction from where I need to go."

"Hush up or I'll send you out to Billy's Island when you get back. They've a new baby, and I want to send over those two little shirts L.B. has outgrown."

Hamp clamped his mouth shut. Billy's Island was half a day west by water.

"I'll go to Scrub's," Neeta said. "I know the way. And I hain't never seen a Negra. Maybe Scrub'll let me peek at 'em."

"Hamp will go with you," Pap said, his voice hard and final. He pushed back from the table and stood haltingly, balancing on his good leg while he fumbled with his crutch. Shook his head before Hamp could say another word. "I don't want no more lip from you, son. You do what your ma and I say do without back talk, or you'll get a backhand to go with it."

Like grease in a pan, anger boiled up in Hamp's chest and threatened to spatter out. Silently he swallowed it, pushed it deep into his gut, down to a place grown so rimed with frost, it couldn't feel such heat.

Thunder rumbled in the distance. Pap ducked his head down quick, as if trying to avoid some invisible thing moving at him through air. He hesitated at the door, his breathing shallow and uneven.

"What is it, Pap?" Neeta asked. "Is there something out there?"

Without turning to look at her, he shook his head and turned away. Hamp stared at Pap's back, so tense that the twin triangles of his shoulder blades nearly touched, drawn up like wings beneath his shirt. He sat down in the slat-backed rocker by the window, and Ma settled L.B. in the crook of his arm. His shoulders slowly relaxed as he rocked back and forth, humming low, his eyes closed.

A tear slid from underneath one of Pap's eyelids and disappeared into the forest of beard that cut beneath the sickle edge of his cheekbone. It'd been so fast, Hamp might have missed it if he hadn't been watching. He felt his face flame from neck to ears, and his spine stiffen. He didn't know Pap anymore. All the swamp had bled out of him up in Tennessee. And from that cold, deep place in the pit of his gut, he couldn't forgive Pap for leaving them and letting it happen.

It would've been easier if he'd died. Easier to bury him and move on than having to live with the goll-darn stranger he'd turned into.

"That's some kind of calaberment, hain't it?" Ma said of a thunder boom that rattled the dishes. "Sounds like the war itself is come down into the swamp this morning."

Hot words spumed up too fast for Hamp to stop. "Well, Pap's the one who helped it find us, Ma. He brought it home with him, didn't he? Damn Yankees, and damn warring outlanders and their damn darkies . . ."

The look on Ma's face poured water on him and locked his jaw. But he couldn't help it. He'd been swallowing hate and anger for so long, it'd filled him up. Had been growing in him like little L.B. had grown inside her, swelling till it nearly crowded out everything else. Sooner or later he wouldn't be able to hold it back. It'd be stronger than he was, with a push of its own.

Before Pap or Ma could jerk him up about the swearing, he scrambled from the table and headed outside. Yessir, he'd go to Scrub's place like they told him. But then he'd do what he wanted—needed—to do. He'd take Bone and get away from Pinder Island. Far away. He didn't care what was out there: Negras, Yankees, hogbears, or the devil himself. He needed to be in the deep swamp where everything was the same as it had always been. But more than anything, he needed to get away from Pap.

Kim L. Siegelson

All morning the sky threatened a freshet. Thunder grumbled and boomed like distant cannon fire. Smoky clouds scudded and roiled overhead, pulsing now and again with lightning. Breathing felt much like pulling air through a damp dishrag, air that had a sharp mineral scent to it, like a gunflint or a grindstone. But the storm drew north and west toward the outlands, and shared not a drop of rain with the swamp. Nothing to pock the sandy dirt in the yard, or quench the planted fields.

Hamp drew up bucket after bucket of water with the long-armed well sweep and filled the three big iron kettles used for washing. As he worked, his anger settled into a quiet smolder like the coals heating the water. Ma and Neeta boiled shirt, diaper, apron and all else in the largest pot. They fished each piece out and rubbed it with a cake of rancid-smelling lye soap, then beat it with a battling stick to loosen the dirt. Hamp noticed that Ma put more vigor in the beating than was usual.

Neeta rinsed the clothes twice, wrung them out and swagged them over bush and fence rail to dry. Hamp could scarcely abide the long wait. He finished most of his day chores and cleaned the mess of warmouths he'd caught earlier. He tried not to think about why he wasn't already deep in the swamp, but every time he looked at

Scrub's britches hanging on the fence or heard Neeta's voice, anger flared up anew.

By the time the dried clothes were gathered and folded, middle day had come and gone, and the light came in slanty-wise through the trees. Hamp sat with Bone on the porch step while Pap played a slow, somber tune on his fiddle and sang:

> "O Polly, O Polly,
> It's for your sake alone,
> I've left my old father,
> My country and my home.
> I've left my old mother
> To weep and to mourn,
> I am a Rebel soldier
> And far from my home."

He said a soldier in his unit had sung it every night in camp for months, a mountain boy who'd sung no more after the first day's battle at Shiloh. Pap played the song over and again till it made Hamp's teeth hurt from the clenching of them.

"Hurry up, Neeta!" he called. Bone jerked his head up off the step at the sharpness in his voice.

Both Neeta and Ma glowered at him, Ma most especially. She put Scrub's bundle of clean clothes in the old croaker sack he'd sent them in, and said, "Neeta, remind Mr. Mooney there'll be a church meeting next month over to Billy's Island. Be a pleasure for him to go along with us if he's a-mind to."

She nodded. "Yes'm, I'll remind him."

As Hamp led her and Bone along the dry trail toward the eastern side of Pinder Island, a pair of nervous woodcocks chortled from the tops of the long-needle pines, and Pap sawed out the opening notes of "Rebel Soldier" yet again.

Bone soon got ahead. He chased gray squirrels through the wiregrass and saw palmetto, and sent them clambering up the tall, scaly trunks of the pines. Neeta walked slow, lagging back to pick a bouquet of meadow beauty, watching little duskywings flit amongst the airy purple flowers. Mostly she jabbered without taking hardly a breath. Trying to draw him out, make him break down and talk.

Well, he'd not speak a word the whole way there and back.

"You ever seen a Negra, Hamp?" she asked, trotting to keep up with him.

He shook his head. Truth was, he knew only what he'd heard.

"They's woolly-headed, and all their skin from head to toe is dark as bog peat," Scrub had said of Negras. "A shim-shacking bunch, crafty and treacherous. Not worth warring over. And I'd surely not leave my wife and babies alone on a farm with the likes of them to go off soldiering. I'd not spill my blood for a one of 'em."

Blood!

Hamp spun around, grabbed Neeta's arm and yanked her to him so hard, she dropped Scrub's clothes and the gathered meadow beauty. Wielding an imaginary knife, he raised his fist over her head and stabbed down at her chest. "All I know about darkies is you can't trust a single one. Deep down, all of 'em is heartless savages, thirsting for blood." He shivered and arranged his face to appear scared. "Lord, I sure hope we don't run into one of the devils. . . ."

He set her loose, pleased at the way she turned wide-eyed and the color blanched from her cheeks. Worth breaking his silence to see. All the rest of the way she followed close on his heels, silent, skittish at every noise in the brush.

As they drew near Scrub's cabin, his three mangy hunting dogs rushed up, baying and barking, but fell off as soon as they recognized Bone. Hamp flinched at the sight of them, too ribby and their ears lumpish with ticks. Fact was, the whole place had a sorry look about it. The yard bristled with vetch and beggar grass, and it stank of old dog piles. Green moss splotched the roof shingles, and dry, brown resurrection fern fringed the splintered edges. Cobwebs festooned windows where Ma would've put up lacy curtains, and three saggy steps led up to a porch stained black with tobacco spit, but for a clean spot beneath the one chair that sat next to the door.

Neeta stopped at the edge of the yard near the smoke-house while Hamp strode forward and banged on Scrub's

Kim L. Siegelson

door. When no one answered, he cracked it and peeked inside. The heavy smell of grease, wood smoke and dirty bed linens drifted out to greet him. "Nobody home," he muttered. A trip for nothing. It didn't surprise him.

"Neeta, just leave the clothes on the chair," he said, pulling the door to. When he turned around, she wasn't where he'd left her.

He found her crouched in the dirt, an ear pressed to the rough wood wall on the backside of the smokehouse, with the four dogs sitting in a watchful half circle around her. She beckoned him, and he squatted beside her and listened to the muffled sounds coming from inside: a child's hiccupy weeping, a woman's voice crooning softly like Ma's when she rocked L.B., a man's low, off-key hum joining in.

"It's them runaways locked in there," Neeta whispered.

The smokehouse walls were solid pine planking, grainy and silver with age. But for two smoke vents and a hinged door, bolted and locked, it hadn't any wall openings. Hamp lay on his belly and peered through a knothole in a low board.

Tepid light seeped in through the smoke vents and gaps between planks, enough so he could see three shadowy figures huddled in a back corner. He pressed in closer and stared at a sweat-slicked man with ropy forearms, and a woman with a graceful neck whose head was bent over a little girl cradled in her lap. Their humming grew quieter as the girl's sobs tapered off. Finally the woman leaned into the man's ribs and closed her eyes.

"Dagg . . . ," Hamp breathed more than spoke. No words came to mind just yet.

"What can you see?" Neeta asked, trying to joog herself in at the knothole.

The woman's eyes opened quick and she sat up straight, startling the girl into a renewed bout of wailing. "Water," she said. "Please, sah, we ain't had no water since yesterdee."

Hamp never had heard such desperate pleading. It froze him.

The man crept over the greasy dirt floor on his hands and knees, then knelt low and braced himself against the wall and put his own eye in line with the knothole. Hamp jerked away from the planks, and Neeta with him. The man felt big and solid. His eyeball gazed out at them. Framed around by splintery wood, it seemed oddly bigger than a normal eye, like a boiled bird egg, shelled and centered with a splot of black pine tar.

"My girl beside herself wit' thirst," the man said, humble-voiced. "Jes' a drop of water for her sho'd be a blessing."

Hamp moved to let Neeta scoot in closer. She put her hand against the wall, as if testing its thickness. Satisfied, she bent level to the eye. "How old is she?"

"Five years come harvest," the man answered. "Born before the war."

Neeta glanced back, smiling, like she wanted Hamp to marvel over her talent for talking to Negras. He mouthed the word *careful* before she turned away.

"Your girl got a name?" she asked.

"Named Mercy, her mama's Ruth, I'm Julius. A man shut us in without food or water—"

"Don't you worry, I'll get you something to drink," Neeta interrupted, patting the wall with her palm in a motherly gesture. She was softhearted about anything she saw as mistreated, always the one to play nurse to the runt piglet of a litter, or scatter an extra measure of cracked corn at the feet of the raggediest hen in the brood.

She hefted Scrub's sack of clothes and trotted to the porch, dogs trailing her. After she set the bundle in the chair by the door, she took a shallow pan that hung from a nail on the wall. Hamp worked the arm of Scrub's well sweep and drew up a bucket of water. He grumbled about it, but truth was, he wouldn't choose to let anybody die of thirst. And it was faster if he helped Neeta. He could still make it to Rooter Island if they hurried.

Neeta dippered water with a gourd ladle and filled the pan. Holding it careful as a silver tray, she trod back across the yard and slid the pan through a slit beneath the smokehouse door. In a moment the girl's crying stopped, replaced by ravenous slurping.

When the empty pan reappeared, both Neeta and Hamp gaped at the sight of the man's hand that had pushed it, for it was near big as a bear's paw, the skin dark as oiled leather but for palm and nail, them being pale as L.B.'s bottom.

Hamp crabbed sideways to retrieve the pan with the

tip of a long stick, wary the hand might take hold of him if he got close again. Neeta took and refilled it, and he pushed it close to the slot with the stick. Over and again the pan emptied and was refilled, until Julius pushed it outside a last time and said, "That's aplenty, thank you."

Neeta found bravery enough to take the pan in hand without aid of a stick. At the door she hunkered back on her heels and squinted close in through a gap. "Did y'all run away from a farm in the outlands?"

"Neeta, I don't have time for you to chat," Hamp said. He'd had enough. The day was slipping away so he'd never get out to Rooter Island.

Neeta ignored him. He heard Ruth and Julius whispering one to the other. "We ain't heard of Outlands," Ruth answered. "The place we left lies aside the Savannah River. Big, pretty farm. Falled on hard times now. Marse and his three boys left two year back, and none is come home yet. Mistus sink down a notch lower every day she don't hear word. I pray for her boys. Then low, she done make some plans to sell me away from my own child. 'I needs money, Ruthie,' she say. . . . Lord best to help her now. I sho' don't want to."

Neeta glanced over her shoulder. Hamp sighed and threw his hands up. He knew the look on her face: pity mixed with the kind of zeal gifted to hard-shell preachers. She stood and rattled the door, as if she expected the rusty key lock caught through the latch to pop free by an act of God.

"Don't send us back," Ruth begged, her voice softer,

hesitant. "Mistus gon' sell me, true. Things been terrible poor since them soldiers come and cleaned out every scrap of food in the smokehouse, the root cellar, the kitchen and the house. Took the chickens, the little pigs, the geese, sheep and beeves. Took the mules and horses, too. All the animal feed. Couldn't nobody stop 'em."

"Held they guns on us," Julius broke in. "Said they'd as soon shoot us as look at us. Nothing to do! No matter how Mistus hollered. No matter she fell down, begging 'em go away. Leave something."

" 'Course you couldn't do nothin'," Neeta said, fiddling with the key lock, her cheeks ruddy with pent-up frustration.

Hamp's own cheeks burned at the thought of their mistress, maybe just like Ma, down on her knees, begging those soldiers to leave. With their guns leveled at her. He shook his head in disgust. "Shows what soulless devils them damn Yankees is," he said. "Robbing a defenseless woman of her food stores. Leaving all to starve. I hope our boys catch them rascals and hang 'em by their toes."

Julius lowered his voice almost to whispering. "These wasn't Yankees. Nawsah, they's Rebel boys. Some of ours. Said they was authorized to take . . . consign, they called it . . . anything they wanted for the use of the Confederate Army."

The lock fell from Neeta's hand and clanked against the latch. She and Hamp stood dumbstruck, with mouths agape.

Hamp found himself before she did. "You're a liar!" he

cried, striding forward to side-kick the smokehouse door. "You're a fork-tongued, lying snake!"

He grabbed Neeta by the back of the collar and hauled her back. She frammed about and kicked at him like a nanny goat, but not before he'd walked her halfway across the yard. He held her at arm's length until she give out of fight.

"Neeta, you've got no business trying to spring that lock. And don't you be jabbering to Ma nor Pap what was said; it hain't true, and lies shouldn't ought to be repeated."

Anger pulled her features toward the center of her face. She fairly hissed at him. "Let me a-loose, Hamp Cravey! You don't know what hain't true and what is."

He let her go, shoved her a half step back in doing so. "Pap was a Confederate soldier. He wouldn't never rob a woman at gunpoint. No Reb would stand for that kind of wrong happening. Least I know that much, and so should you. It's proof you can't trust nothing a darkie says. Nothing!"

Scrub was right about them.

He turned his back on Neeta and on the smokehouse, quiet now but for the sound of Mercy whining of hunger, pleading at her ma to open the door.

It was too late to make a start for Rooter Island now. Too much time wasted watering a darkie snake and listening to his passel of lies. Hamp put his fingers to his lips and whistled for Bone, long and hard. Whistled till the blood hammered hot behind his eye sockets. The shrillness of it shushed the bird twitter and drowned out the little girl's voice.

All the long way home he walked fast, and Neeta followed without lagging. She didn't chatter on like before. But to Hamp there was no peace in her quiet. No peace in his own, either. It seemed like a pause, like the brief, heavy stillness that came over the swamp just before a rainstorm.

Chapter 4

Neeta held to her ponderous silence through the day, which stayed gray with linty clouds so low slung, they seemed liable to snag in the crowns of the tallest pines. At early evenfall she and Hamp drove the cows home from their foraging. He tried to josh her out of her glum mood, and then reason with her.

"Them runaways hain't worth your worry, Neeta. Scrub's the one to get paid for catching them. Let him fret."

But she'd not budge, speaking most powerfully with glares and scowls.

Ma took such low funk for spring sickness, several

times touching the backs of her fingers to Neeta's forehead for sign of fever. She brewed a pot of sage tea and sweetened it with a drop of cane syrup and had Neeta sip on a steaming cupful as remedy for the ailment.

As Hamp had asked, she'd not spoken about Scrub's runaways to Ma and Pap other than to say it was plumb cruel for Scrub to lock them up without food nor water to drink. And she mentioned how the woman claimed to pray for the sons of her mistress, off warring, maybe killed. Before she could tell the rest, Hamp cleared his throat and coughed till Ma fetched a cup of tea for him, too.

'Twas brooding, not fever, that ailed Neeta. Hamp knew so, for he felt sick with it himself. He could not rid himself of what Julius had said. He could not keep himself from imagining Ma on hands and knees, pleading while soldiers in gray stole everything they owned. And each one looked like Pap . . .

Tired of thinking, Hamp turned in early. He slept but a few fitful hours before waking. He lay abed wide-eyed in the dark, listening to the hollow, lift-and-wane music the wind-stirred tree boughs played. Almost like a lullaby—a sad one. It conjured to mind once again Julius and Ruth and Mercy, huddled together in shadow so that three appeared to be only one. And the one sang a mother's song.

He clamped his eyes shut and covered his ears. "Forget their lies," he told himself. "Forget about them."

Kim L. Siegelson

Finally sleep folded over him, this time nightmarish and dry as a jackdaw's wing. He found himself lost in the deep swamp. A monstrous hogbear stalked him, its girth bigger around than a full-grown ox bull. With no aim but to get away, he ran and ran for what seemed like miles. Yet no matter how fast he churned his legs, or how far he traveled, the monster followed close behind, lumbering through the trees, yellow eyes glowing fierce as pine-knot torches.

He fired on it with a musket, but the lead slug glanced off, skipping the way stones on water will. He came to a cow house and with heart pounding his ribs, climbed to the roof. As the bear drew near, it stretched up with sudden growth till it reached level with the roof eaves. Three heads reared up on its shoulders, each with a gaping maw that stank of rot, and every tooth gleaming long and sharp as a polished iron spike.

Whimpering, he scrabbled to gain purchase on the pitched roof, digging nail and toe into the crannies between overlapped shingles. But all was slickened with green moss, and he only skiddered closer to the monster for all his effort. Suddenly a machete blade came into his hand by way of miracle or feverish hope. He gripped it two-fisted, chopping vicious strokes as if clearing heavy brush from a trail, while rump sliding toward the drop-off.

Thwack! Metal blade met fur and flesh and neck bone, carving through with one hard stroke. A severed head toppled from the monster's shoulders while the two living heads howled. Hamp and the lopped head landed side by side in the dirt. The blood-clotted blade turned to brittle ash in his hands.

Before he could catch his wind, the head fixed its blazing eyes on him and with vinelike sprouting pushed forth arms and legs and trunk, thickening and reaching toward the sky until it stood whole beside the other.

He cowed against the cow-house wall and screamed, "Pap! Pap!"

He woke trembling and sweat-chilled, his hair and nightshirt soaked through, his bed linens knotted round his legs. Soon as he began to ease, the dogs took up bawling at some night critter in the yard. The sound cranked his heart high up in his throat again, froze him. Any other night he'd have troubled himself to throw off covers and peep out, but he couldn't now. Ma would, or Pap.

Soon he heard the cabin door open and close.

He dozed after that but did not sleep again for fear of dreaming. He rose at first light when Ma got up with L.B., and sat with her while she pared yams and put them to boil for breakfast.

"You look pale as raw dough," she said, and set L.B. on his lap to pour him a draught of cold tonic in a cup.

"Ma, do you think dreams have meanings?" he asked over the cup rim.

"I don't know, Hamp. Your gre-granpap said he'd had a few that foretold of later happenings."

Hamp shivered at the thought.

Kim L. Siegelson

All the morning, he hung close to the house. Whenever he thought on the hogbear dream, his insides washed toward his knees. It shamed him that he'd cried out for Pap in his sleep like a hen-hearted coward. Shamed him that such a thing was keeping him from checking his traps out on Rooter Island like he wanted. Disgusted with himself, he scrubbed his clammy palms against the seat of his britches and sank down onto the porch bench.

He glowered across the yard at Neeta and Pap. She sat side-straddle on the top fence rail, leaning forward, and braced by one hand on the post head. One bare foot swung in lazy to-and-fro arcs while she watched Pap tinker with the hog-pen gate. She pointed and said something. Pap grinned before he answered her, and their heads tipped closer together while he talked and daubed grease on the hinge pintle.

Anger buzzed at the back of Hamp's mind. Pap didn't talk to him with such ease anymore. Now that he'd grown big enough to look Pap straight in the eye, neither of them ever did. They looked away, or stared at the ground or the sky when they spoke at all.

A row of six beegums lined the far southerly end of the fence. Sun-warmed bees seethed from around the edges of the shingle and lifted up bright and quick as sparks from a chimney stack. Hamp gathered his knees in with his arms and pondered how far they might have to fly in search of one drop of flower nectar, how dangerous.

Yet time and again they darted away from their safe, warm hive. And there he sat, afeared of dream monsters like a shim-shacking fool while the day slipped by.

He unfolded his legs and fixed his mind toward getting trumpery and food together and setting out for Rooter like he should've earlier. But soon as he got to his feet, Bone and Rascal tore out from under the porch and across the yard to the line where clearing met denser brush. Stiff-legged and aquiver, they yammered and bawled until Pap scolded them to shush up. In a moment Scrub hallooed from a-ways off as signal to expect him coming.

When finally he pushed through the limbs of gallberry and myrtle at the head of the path, three soldiers followed close behind him.

Quickly Hamp rose from the step into a half crouch. If these were raiders, he could take two steps and reach the musket just inside the cabin door.

He took quick measure of them. They looked to be his elders by no more than a handful of years. All three wore Confederate uniforms: two had britches of butternut brown and checkered shirts of different shades; the third wore tatty gray britches and a linen shirt that might've been white at one time before it'd been washed with lampblack.

The one in gray was the tallest of the three and strode forward in a long ham-knocker coat of the same cloth as his britches, his hat a slumped sugarloaf crown banded with salt rings of new and old sweat. The wide, soft brim

Kim L. Siegelson

cast his eyes in shade. Hamp figured him to be the leader, for he walked ahead of the other two and seemed on the verge of barking orders.

The two in butternut sported smaller, flattened caps that looked like tin pots mashed down atop their heads. One man had a wide, almost lipless mouth with long, thready whiskers at the corners like a catfish. The other man had a baby's round, pink face, and his eyes, nose and mouth were clustered tight at its center.

Pap fought with men like these, Hamp told himself. He stood up straight and respectful, though uneasiness still pricked at him.

Rascal and Bone took to yipping again as the strangers drew nearer, lunging and growling at them. In a blink, the man in the coat kicked out and caught Rascal under the chin with the toe of his boot, lifting him up off his front paws and throwing him on his back. Hamp leapt past the last step into the yard before he stopped. Pap would take up for Rascal, cuss the man a blue streak, clop him with his cane. "Pap!" he called out, wanting to stop him. Worried what might happen next.

But Pap didn't cuss the soldier. Only the smallest cloud passed over his face as he took up his crutch and hobbled out to greet the strangers.

Rascal scrabbled in the dirt, and then, tail-tucked and yelping, he ran to his hidey place under the porch with Bone at his heels. Hamp wished he could hide, too, rather than watch Pap shake hands with such a one as that. Ma and Neeta joined him on the porch. Ma wet her fingers with her tongue and raked them through his hair to tame it. As the men drew nearer, all snatched their hats from their heads and held them pinchered by the brim in front of them. Three limp swamp rabbits dangled by their ears from Scrub's fist. He swung them in the direction of the man in the coat and said, "Mrs. Cravey, this here's Lieutenant Angus Tate, come down from Macon."

Ma worried her hands together at her waist. "Is the war reached this far south then, Lieutenant? Are we to be expecting bluecoats soon?"

Hamp felt his gut coil into knots, but he couldn't stop from smiling at Neeta's face, suddenly bleached pale as a tallow candle.

Lieutenant Tate pulled his lips tight across his teeth and shook his head. "No, ma'am, I don't believe the Yanks will make it past Atlanta." He paused to tip his chin at the other men. "But there's a certain Negra boy we've been trailing all the way from Rockyface near to Dalton, a darkie mean and two-faced as they come. Been sidestepping us for nearly seven weeks, but if it's the last thing I do on God's earth, I'll hunt him down, and . . ." His voice faltered and his face twisted as if he'd tasted some nastiness. Neeta scooted closer to Ma. The two other soldiers hung their heads and fidgeted with their hats. Hamp thought suddenly of Julius and felt a quick pang of worry pulse through him.

Scrub splumed a hearty stream of amber tobacco juice from between his teeth with force enough to notch a hole in the dirt next to the steps. "The darkie killed the lieutenant's brother in cold blood, Mrs. Cravey, and he's not got over it."

Ma touched her fingertips to her mouth in the gesture of prayer, and lowered her eyes. "No, I don't expect he has," she said softly. "Well, least we can do is feed you. You boys will stay and take a meal, won't you?"

"Some rabbit stew would sure be fine," Scrub said, his smile a misery of bad teeth. "As the hired guide and master tracker of this hunt party, I say we've got time for it."

Pap cleared his throat and rubbed the back of his neck. "Scrub, hain't you got some Negras locked up at your place right now?"

"Three, but nary a one of them the boy we's looking for," Scrub answered, spraying droplets of brown spittle onto his shirtfront.

Hamp heard Neeta let her breath out. His own relief surprised him.

"I put a bucket of water and some feed in with them," Scrub went on, "but I wager the reward for catching the lieutenant's boy is bigger than what I'd get for them three put together."

Tate swiped the back of his hand across his eyes and under his nose. "My father is offering five hundred dollars in gold coin for capture of the wretched boy. So's we may have the pleasure of serving what justice he deserves."

Five hundred dollars! Hamp could scarcely imagine such a sum.

He conjured a clear picture of what awaited the boy, for Tate had already strangled his poor hat halfway to death. But the idea of having that much money in gold coin made him feel fainty, and deeply hungry. With gold it didn't matter which side won the war, Federal or Confederate, for its worth wasn't tied to either flag. Not like money printed on paper.

Five hundred dollars was riches beyond hoping for, and it soured his stomach to think of Scrub filling his money box with coins while theirs stayed empty as a dried-up mud dauber nest.

Ma put her hand on his shoulder and squeezed it. "Fetch me a scoop of cracked corn from the shed to make parched-corn coffee, Hamp, and a thumb-sized piece of salt pork from the smokehouse. I expect Pap and Scrub and the soldiers will talk over the best way to search."

Hamp nodded, and shrugged her hand away. He squatted beside the steps and patted his leg until Bone belly-crawled from shadows. Rascal wouldn't budge. He stayed hunkered inside the dirt hollow he'd dug out as his bed, blinking at Hamp, his sore muzzle resting atop his paws.

Hamp understood, for he felt like he'd had the air kicked out of him, too. Why did someone like Scrub have all the luck? God wasn't paying close attention to what was fair.

Bone trailed him across the yard to the shed, set between the corncrib and smokehouse. Ma's favorite cow, Sugarlump, stood with her rump nearly blocking the door, pulling dry husks through the gaps between the logs of the corncrib. She caught wind of Bone and stamped her back hoof anxiously.

Kim L. Siegelson

Hamp ran his hand along her wide, dusty flank as he squeezed past her, and crooned, "Easy, girl, easy." But Bone darted between her legs and rammed his muzzle under the shed door, tore at the dirt with his claws and growled. Sugarlump startled and backed her hindquarters up until her tail whipped Hamp in the face and about the shoulders.

"Daggit, Bone! Stop!" he yelled. Shut-eyed against the tail switching, he fumbled for the latch and tripped it. Soon as the door swung in, Bone burst through. Following behind, he slammed it shut to keep the cow from following. Why the devil was Bone acting so fitful? It gave him a jumpy feeling so that he moved slowly, carefully. Looking out for something, but he didn't know what.

Cypress boards and oak-staved barrels scented the cool darkness inside with the sharp, sappy smell of a forest. Beams a-glitter with dust spirals slantered between the jam of wall and roof, throwing broken shards of light on the earthen floor. Pale clay crocks squatted toadlike among the barrels, and smaller crocks and jars lined sagging shelves fixed between the wall frames. Everything in place, same as always.

But it felt wrong. As if the air were turning in a different direction, ruffling up the hairs on Hamp's arms. He rubbed his hands over them and watched Bone snuffling a trail through the dirt, jooging his nose into every corner, sucking in deep snorting breaths.

"What's eating you, Bone?" he whispered. "I don't see nothing but mouse droppings and last season's taters." He bent to look more closely at the floor. There were many footprints: starry little mouse tracks, the blunt-toed prints made by dog pads, the large curve and dot pattern made by human feet.

One print caught his eye. A fresh human footprint perfectly pressed into a dark, oily patch of floor. Something not right. He caught Bone by the scruff of his neck and counted the toes. ". . . Three, four, five, six."

He looked at his own feet and knew without counting that he had five on each one. So did Ma, and Pap, and Neeta, and even L.B., who couldn't walk yet. Nobody on Pinder Island had six toes. Not even Scrub.

He let go of Bone and stood stock-still, looked around with a hunter's eyes, more careful now. A rusty pail was missing from its hook. Snagged on the tip of a broken barrel stave was a torn strip of dirty homespun cloth the size of a hair ribbon. Behind the barrel a large sack of dry corn lay flat on a wood riser, gaped open at the center, raggedly split from top to bottom with some sort of blade. Loose kernels spilled out of the gash in a scatter across the dirt.

He remembered how Bone and Rascal had howled so during the night. Not at a raccoon, nor possum, then, but at a thief. One who carried a blade. He knew he should run and tell Pap and Ma, but a thought held him frozen. What if the thief was the Negra boy who'd killed Tate's brother?

His heart clanged behind his breastbone to think it. And think, too, that he could be the one to track the boy down and bring him in. Get the five hundred in gold coin for himself. He was a better tracker than Scrub, even Pap'd said so. He need only keep quiet about the signs, let Scrub lead the soldiers away, then follow the trail on his own. With trembling hands he unsnagged the bit of cloth, filled a empty tin with loose corn for Ma and called Bone out of the shed behind him.

A nesting jackdaw shrieked warning from the eave of the cow house and swooped down at Bone, but he paid it no mind. He stared off into the brush, splay-legged and tight as a metal coil, sensing a trail only dogs could understand.

Hamp forced himself to walk, not run, to the smokehouse. Once inside he shallowed his breathing, not only at the smell of rancid meat drippings and soured wood ash, but from edginess, too. He unwrapped a square of oily hemp cloth that bound the slab of salt pork and took its measure; it was smaller by half than just two days earlier. If Ma found out, she'd be sick about it. But he'd not tell her yet. Not till he had the five hundred in gold. He could nearly feel the weight of it in his hands, and hear the jingling sound it would make.

He opened his folding knife and carved a waxy hunk of meat from one side of the pork, hesitated, and then took a second piece. He tore a strip from the hemp cloth and bound the second hunk with it, and shoved it into his pocket for traveling food. The rest he rewrapped. It wasn't stealing, not really. Anyway, he'd make up for it when he got the reward money.

Turning round, he spied a dozen six-toed prints in the

salty film that glazed the hard-packed earthen floor. Saw upon looking down that his own foot had landed squarely atop one—his size, and strangely warm, as if fresh enough to still hold some body heat of the one who'd made it. He pressed his full weight down on it and gripped his toes in, working to suppose a brown face to match it. None came, except the faces of Julius and Ruth. But they were a family, this boy was a murderer.

He pushed his thoughts away from them, turned and trod heavily over the trail of footprints, masking them with his own. Outside he scuffed the traces of salt from his soles while the jackdaw swooped and scolded Bone, a fury of black feathers.

Chapter 5

M a insisted on boiling the soldiers' filthy clothes while the rabbit stew cooked, and would not listen to argument that they'd be collecting new dirt as soon as they took to the swamp. Finally Tate looked down at himself and then at his men, and turned red about the ears. "Living with nothing but men, you stop noticing how ripe you've gotten," he said. "And stop caring. My mother would be fitified to see me so low slung."

"I believe she'd be nothing but pleased to see you," Ma answered, "and it's my pleasure to offer what comfort to you boys as I can." She drew up stiff-spined and waved off any more arguments. Soon as she was out of earshot, the boy with catfish whiskers nicknamed her The General.

So it was with sour mood that Hamp set to filling the wash kettles with water for the second time in two days. He knew what he wanted to do—take Bone and light out for the swamp, follow the trail of the thief while it was fresh. As the arm of the well sweep levered up and down and he toted bucket after bucket of water, he fought to keep himself steady, keep his plans hidden. He wanted Scrub and Tate to go away quick.

For the life of him he couldn't see why Ma had her mind so fixed on cleanliness. By the way Neeta huffed off to fetch the soap and washboard and battling stick, he knew she felt the same way.

Tate had stayed back to help kindle fire beneath the largest of the iron pots. When flames licked up good and hot, he fetched a tin plate from his pack and bid Hamp over. "Ever seen a Rebel mule race?" he asked, squatting beside the fire.

"Nosir," Hamp answered. He hunkered down beside Tate, curious.

Tate laid the plate on the ground, then dug at the back of his grimy collar and along his hairline. In a moment he brought pinchered fingers close to the plate and dropped at its center two fat graybacks the size of turnip seeds. The lice seemed unable to fathom the sudden change in scenery from dark forest of hair to bare metal desert. Addled, they crawled a tight circle in opposite directions till they bumped heads together where they'd first started.

Tate pointed at the smaller of the two lice and said, "I wager a copper he'll be the one that reaches the edge of the plate first."

"If I had one, I might wager," Hamp answered.

Tate nodded. "Fair enough. They'll race without wager." Carefully he held most of the plate over the edge of the fire. As the tin heated, the two graybacks began to scramble a determined line toward cooler ground, their tiny legs moving with more speed than Hamp thought possible. He and Tate beat their palms on their knees and cheered when, sure enough, the smaller one reached the raised edge first.

Tate raised an eyebrow at Hamp and then tipped the plate forward so that both racers tumbled into the flames. Two quick pops followed by two bright sparks ended them. For a moment neither Hamp nor Tate spoke. Then Tate said, "Why don't you get a colored boy or gal to do your water toting and fire tending and such?"

Hamp frowned and poked at the fire with a stick. "We can do for ourselves."

"Anyone can, but the darkies was put here to serve and work, so I say let them do what they was made for. Back home, we have more than two hundred head of them."

"I expect you don't even have to lift your hand to wipe your own nose, huh?" Hamp asked, scorn making his voice sound sharp. "Way I hear it, they's more trouble than they're worth."

Tate dug again at his scalp and flicked the pickings into the heat. Steam had begun to scroll up from the surface of the pot, and when he let out a breath, it jerked aside like a living thing. "Maybe, but I don't like thinking what it'd be like if we didn't have them. Most coloreds is faithful and true as hounds. Docile once you gain their respect and learn to handle them. Sometimes a high idea will come into one of their woolly heads and brew up trouble. This war and foolish talk of elevating the Negra has sown fancy notions in too many of them. Makes some think they ought to run off from their owners, even turned a few to violence."

"That right?" Hamp said. He thought of Julius's weight pressing against the smokehouse wall—a dangerous strength.

Tate narrowed his eyes and scoured the back of his neck with his hand as he continued talking. "None of us guessed Duff would do what he done to my brother Gavin. Eats me up just to think of it."

"Duff is the boy you're hunting?"

"He's the son of Gavin's wet nurse," Tate said, nodding. "About a year older. The two of them grew up alongside each other, close as kin. Closer than what's proper, to my thinking.

"Gavin always begged Daddy not to sell Duff, never to send him away, so when Gavin turned twelve, Daddy gifted Duff to him so as he'd stop pestering him about the boy at every turn. He swore he'd live to regret giving Gavin such a strong-willed buck as Duff. Said he had the devil in him and Gavin hadn't the heart to break him properly or master him.

"Turned out to be true. Duff never learned his place. He looked you right in the eye, and talked so proper you'd think he'd been schooled. Most uppity-acting darkie I ever met."

Hamp tapped the stick against the side of the pot while Tate paused to stare up at a flock of ricebirds flitting among the low boughs of a persimmon tree. When Tate spoke again, it seemed like he was talking to himself, or maybe the birds.

"Mother tried to stop me and Gavin from joining up to fight in the war. But neither him nor me wanted to sit home like milksops, and Daddy agreed we ought to go. He's seen Yankee cities, and says they're crowded stink holes full of foreigners and roughnecks, beggars and tainted women. He told Mother we must do all we can to stop such filth from infecting the South.

"Of course, when Duff found out, he wouldn't hear of Gavin going without him. Mother agreed he should go. I think she hoped he'd keep Gavin out of danger, protect him somehow. She couldn't have been more wrong. Duff fooled us all."

"He killed Gavin," Hamp blurted, repeating what Scrub had said earlier. Only now the words made him burn with outrage.

Tate gestured at the barn. "Them two boys with me? They served in Gavin's company. Told how he was wounded during a skirmish with the Yanks outside Crow Valley. And they seen Duff run to him under fire and drag him safe into a stand of saplings. But next time one of them looked, he seen Gavin and Duff arguing. Gavin cussing Duff something fierce. A minute later Duff had a gun, kneeling before Gavin with the barrel pointed close at his face. Before a one of them could rise up and defend my brother, artillery hit close and sent them ducking.

"When all was over with and the battle ended, they found Gavin in the thicket right where Duff left him. Half his head was missing. Duff was gone."

Hamp winced like he'd been punched. He couldn't think what to say.

Tate picked up a hunk of wood and chucked it up at the ricebirds. They took to wing in a like-minded surge, the way a shoal of minnows will move as one body through the water. Bright, hidden patches of scarlet feathers flashed as they beat their black wings.

"My company wasn't far away, so I asked furlough and hired a wagon and took Gavin home. When I told what'd happened, Daddy bid Duff's mama to come to him. I've never seen him in such rage, never seen him raise a hand to any servant, but on that day he flailed her. Beat her with a strap till he tore her clothes to flinders and cut her skin. Mother wrenched it from his hand and begged him stop. She said to let God take vengeance as He saw fit."

"My ma would say the same," Hamp offered. He didn't say he thought only a hardhearted man would whip a woman, even a slave woman.

"Well, I can't wait for God's vengeance!" Tate spat the words out in a spray of spittle that sizzled on the side of the iron kettle. "Duff is a traitorous black-hearted Judas, and he'll pay for his sin by my hand, with his blood. No easy death, neither. Nosir, he'll suffer. And so will every traitorous runaway darkie I find." His voice hitched and he turned his face up toward the smutty clouds and clenched his lids tight over his eyes. His jaw muscles twitched with the rhythm of chewing. "That's my promise to Gavin," he whispered.

Chapter 6

Hamp's belly felt knotted as a lanyard. He was certain now he couldn't go live outside the swamp, among a mess of outlanders and darkies. Nosir. He wanted that bounty money. More than anything he wanted it. He shoved his stick into the fire and rose to his feet. "How would I know this boy if I was to come upon him?" he asked, careful not to sound eager, just interested.

"Easy as counting toes," Tate answered. He opened his eyes, now pink-stained slits center-set with chips of cold blue ice. "Duff's got six digits on the left foot. He's seventeen years old, not tall, skin color like a brown onion husk."

"All right," Hamp said with a quick nod. He thought of the prints in the shed, and figured each toe to be worth a gold piece. The urge to start hunting the boy nearly overwhelmed him. He stood and excused himself, mumbling about getting to his chores.

But an unasked question stopped him. He scratched the back of his ankle with his toe, looking for the right words. "I've heard about Confederates raiding farms. Hain't it just Yankees doing such?"

Tate glared at him, his face ablaze with new anger. "Yankees is like pirates, son. They raid and plunder, strip a place cleaner than locusts swarming down on a field of grain. They take ladies' dresses for saddle blankets, crush babies' toys under their boots, family dogs are shot out of meanness, loyal servants kidnapped, and lastly the house and ever last outbuilding is put to the torch. Pirates!"

He paused, then lowered his voice. "Of course, when the supply lines is cut off or slowed down by the bluecoats, our own troops might be forced to take some food and animals and fodder, consign is the word for it. We've got to have supplies to keep going. But we surely don't burn folks out in the end. And there's the difference in it, don't you see."

Hamp bobbed his head in a show of understanding,

but found himself tongue-tied yet again, stumped for words. Bruised-hearted, he left Tate to himself. Whatever Julius was, he wasn't a liar.

Hamp thought about that all the rest of the afternoon while he piddled at chores, mostly around the cow house so he'd be within earshot of Scrub and the soldiers, who were naked and waiting inside until their clothes dried.

He heard Scrub say they'd head west toward Billy's Island directly after supper. Ma'd seen signs that someone had traveled through in that direction, and they might find a few more men on Billy's for the hunt. Using punt boats, they'd make good time on water and get there before nightfall.

Hamp was relieved they'd be going west, because the trail he'd take led south. No chance of crossing paths. He puzzled over what signs Ma had seen. Why didn't she mention them earlier to him or Pap? Well, it didn't matter. When it came to tracking and reading signs, he trusted Bone and his own eyes more than anything or anyone, including Scrub and Ma.

Only Pap had more skill, but Pap didn't count any-more.

The prints in the smokehouse and shed were Duff's, no question, and Bone scented his trail going south, toward Rooter. Into the part of the swamp that was his, the prairie heads and cypress bays he best knew, that he had hunted for as long as he could remember. Catching Duff would be easy as spotting a firefly in the dark.

The sun burned off most of the cloud cover by mid-

Kim L. Siegelson

dle day. Shadows reached across the open flats and lengthened, the puddled blots of shade at the foot of the trees unfurling like fingers from a closed fist.

Instead of lunch, Ma served an early supper of rabbit stew and corn pone and parched-corn coffee. Tate and the other two soldiers shoveled food down their gullets like they'd not eaten since the start of the war. Though their shirts and britches were still damp at the waist and collars and cuffs, Tate said they did appreciate wearing clothes cleaned of the reek of the battlefield and the traveling.

Pap didn't eat. He sipped corn coffee and played "Rebel Soldier" on the fiddle, pulling his bow over the strings so it brought to mind a woman's voice a-keening and weeping and praying. But he wouldn't sing the words. Tate asked if he knew them, and he lied and said, "Did once, but no more."

Finally the last bit from the stew pot was scraped up and eaten, and the kettle drained of every drop of coffee. The soldiers gathered their packs and other trumpery together and followed Scrub through the lower fields to the landing. Hamp and Neeta watched them load up, two to a punt: Scrub and Tate in Scrub's boat, Tate's men in Pap's. In a squirt Scrub's punt skimmed a smooth line over Pinder Lake. The second boat waggled and jerked a jagged path, struggling to keep up with Scrub's lead.

Neeta giggled to see it flounder so. "I don't think a one of them soldiers ever held a paddle afore. But they best be careful about staying up close or everybody'll be out hunting for them."

Hamp smiled, but his mind churned with plans. Now he could go. Finally. He'd wait for night, then foot his way through the swamp. It'd be harder without the punt. Trails might be dry or wet, open or tangled. What trumpery and food he took he'd have to carry. It'd not be much. Bone and the musket were the only things he couldn't do without. Pap forbade him from taking the musket from the house, and if he dared ask, Ma would catch on and forbid him from leaving Pinder Island. But they'd both be glad when he collected that bounty money. He'd take the musket—no, he'd *consign* it. And they'd forgive him for sneaking off in the dark of night. They'd understand.

Night seeped in from the trees like spilled inkberry juice. Hamp lay abed with his eyes wide open, his fingers knitted together over his belly. He watched the half-moon untangle itself from the pines and climb the sky, wishing it could move faster. He listened at the whistling trill of tree peepers and the throaty burps of bullfrogs and wondered on what Duff was doing. Wondered if he was awake, out in the swamp watching the same moon, feeling safe in his hiding place. Was he proud of the evil he'd done? Or sorry? Did he pray not to be caught?

Hamp closed his eyes and prayed it'd be him to catch Duff.

Finally he unfolded his fingers from over his belly and eased up. His heart jangled behind his ribs as he crept down the ladder from the sleeping loft and tippy-toed past Ma's and Pap's bed. With breath held, he lifted

Kim L. Siegelson

the musket from its spot near the door, hefted the shot bag from its hook and slipped outside. Bone raised himself from his spot on the porch and followed him along the side yard until they reached the shed.

Hamp eased the door open a crack, knelt and reached inside for the pack he'd left there, slung it over his back. Crickets and frogs chirred and garumped with noise enough to cover the patter of his feet on the dirt as he slunk toward the outhouse. A chuck-will's-widow cried out its name three times and fell silent. Wouldn't I make a right fine spy, he thought as he slid along the outhouse sidewall, mouth-breathing to keep the stench from burning his nose.

The outhouse door swung open beside him with such suddenness, he nearly dropped the musket. Rusty hinges screeched loud as a barn owl, and acrid air whooshed out as Neeta stepped from inside. Hamp flattened himself into what shadow he could. Pressed the blades of his shoulders into the rough planks, sucked in his breath and held it.

Bone didn't. He trotted forward and pushed his muzzle into Neeta's hand. She stood still, patting his head. Listening. He saw her straining to hear. Waiting.

Satisfied with Neeta's petting, Bone trotted back to join Hamp. Neeta followed him. Her eyes narrowed when she spied Hamp. In the ashy light her face had the sly, pointed appearance of a lizard. "Where do you think you're going to with that musket, Hamp Cravey?" she whispered.

He reached out and yanked her closer toward him, clamped a hand over her mouth, and then dragged her down the path that led to the deep swamp before he spoke. "Are you trying to wake up all creation? I'm getting a early start at hunting is all," he whispered.

"Middle night's mighty early," she said, her voice sharp as catbrier thorns. "And you hain't to take that musket. Pap said so!"

Before he could answer, she leaned in and whispered, "You're planning to go find that boy who killed Tate's brother, hain't you? Ma and Pap'll be madder than scorched hornets when they find out."

Hamp grabbed her wrist and dug his fingers in. "You better not go tattling, Neeta."

"Maybe I won't," she said, jerking her hand free of him, "if you help me do something first."

Hamp groaned and gritted his teeth. "What?"

"Scrub might be gone a long time with them soldiers. Help me get them people out of his smokehouse. I can't do it by myself."

"Daggit, Neeta! I told you that's none of our business!" There was more certainty in Hamp's voice than he felt in his heart. The sound of Mercy crying of thirst still tugged at him. Scrub treated his dogs poorly, and he probably thought less about how Negras was kept. . . .

"What if they don't have enough to drink and eat, Hamp?" Neeta insisted. "What if they was to die in there and we let it happen? All they done wrong was run

52   Kim L. Siegelson

off and steal their own selves. Tell me how stealing your-self is evil enough to die for."

" 'Cause there's a law says if you're a slave, you can't steal yourself. And another says anyone who helps slaves run is a thief."

"That's plumb addle-headed and you know it," Neeta hissed, jabbing him in the center of his chest with her finger.

Hamp blew out a heavy sigh and shook his head. He was losing time. "Neeta . . ."

She glared at him, her eyes hard as iron slugs and a-glint with cold moonlight. Quick as a viper she struck out and grabbed the musket midbarrel. "A stupid law! Now, help me or I'll holler for Ma and Pap."

He opened his mouth but couldn't argue. They both knew it. Neeta was harder to budge than Sugarlump at the corncrib when she got her mind set on a thing. With every passing minute Duff's trail grew staler. And at first light he'd be moving again.

"I don't like the idea of busting Scrub's smokehouse door down," Hamp grumbled. "Bad enough to break the law by helping them fugitives escape. And how are we to keep Scrub's dogs from chasing them folks once we get the door open?"

Bone noozled in between him and Neeta. She let go the musket and took a step back. "They'll be no busting doors, Hamp. And I got a idea for them hounds. Wait here while I run back to the shed." At the head of the path she stopped and turned around, cupped her hands round her mouth and whisper-yelled, "If you leave without me, you'll be sorrier than a possum down a well."

"I'm already sorry," Hamp muttered.

Chapter 7

It was nearly too dark to see the trail through the pine woods and saw palmettos. Droplets of water clung to the business ends of the sharp-tipped leaves, shining in the brittle moonlight like quicksilver dripped onto the tips of needles and bayonets. Thick fog had gathered into shifting, knee-deep pools that fooled Hamp's eye into doubting the solid nature of the ground.

Every footstep, he took on faith, from memory.

Bone seemed not to have such doubts. He capered through the brush with ease, for long minutes disappearing into the gray swirl so that only the crackle and snap of twigs told where he might be, then with phantom stealth darted out again. He'd hang close for a while, noozle the trail and vanish again into the wisp.

Neeta moved faster than Hamp thought she could, like someone had lit a pine-knot torch under her rump.

He shifted his pack to his other shoulder and adjusted the gun and shot-bag straps. Trotted to keep up with her even though she carried a weighty haversack slung over her shoulder.

Neither of them spoke much, though they'd got far enough from the cabin not to be heard by Ma or Pap. When they did speak, their voices were muffled and strange. Hamp likened it to having bits of cotton wadding stuffed in his ears, and thought to tell Neeta, but didn't. The quiet suited him, and left his ears open to other sounds: Bone's romping, the chirruping of bats, his own breath and Neeta's, the clink of the gun barrel against a pack buckle. And should there be a sound that didn't belong to them or the swamp, he'd hear it.

When they reached the edge of Scrub's yard, his pack of dogs fell on them, tussling and lunging and rearing up to snap at the haversack Neeta carried. She dug inside and pulled a smaller croaker sack from it, and then from inside it one of the rabbit skins from those Scrub had brought for making stew.

"Here, dogs," she called out. In a tangle of legs and tails they swarmed closer around her skirt hem. Bone danced in the thick of them, and Hamp grabbed him by the nape of his neck and hauled him back. Neeta lifted the fresh hide high overhead as she led the rest of the pack across the yard and up the cabin steps to the porch. She pulled the front door open wide, and with a quick flick, flung the skin into the cabin. The dogs raced after it in a wild scramble, fell on it in a snarling knot. While they played tug-o-war, Neeta slammed the door on them and wedged the porch chair up under the handle.

Hamp let a smile pull at the corners of his mouth. "You know they'll mess the floor."

"Scrub won't notice it if they do," she said, wiping her hands on the front of her cotton shift. She took up the haversack from where she'd dropped it, fetched from it Pap's clawed hammer and a long, thick nail and toted them to the smokehouse.

She tapped on the door with her knuckles. "You awake in there? It's Neeta and Hamp. Come to get you out."

Surprised cries came from inside the smokehouse: "Thy God Almighty!" and "Glory!"

Hamp took a deep breath and pushed in front of Neeta. He gripped her shoulders to hold her back. "We shouldn't ought to do this. If we set about freeing Negras, don't you think it'll put us on level with Yankees and trai-tors?"

"No, I don't think it," she answered, shrugging his hands away. "Setting three runaways a-loose don't lessen my hate of Yankees. They invaded us first and I hope our boys whoop 'em for it."

Hamp stepped aside reluctantly. "All right, I'll help you break in. But don't expect no more of me past that. Once out, they're on their own."

Neeta squatted down and fitted the pointed end of the nail in the notch at the bottom of the hinge where the pintle fit into the gudgeon socket. She gave it two sharp

Kim L. Siegelson

raps with the hammer so that the pintle jacked upward, then gripped the head of it with the claw end of the hammer and tugged. The dogs inside the cabin yammered and bawled at the shrill skreaking of it being levered free.

"Where'd you learn that trick, Neeta?" he wondered aloud. Thought to himself she might not be so pea-brained after all.

"Watching Pap fix the pigpen gate." She passed the hammer and nail to him. "Now you do the top one. It's too high for me."

He drove the second pintle up and yanked it out. No longer fastened at the gudgeons, the hinges separated into halves. With Julius pushing and Hamp pulling, the door cracked open at the hinge breaks. Ruth and Mercy squeezed through first, followed by Julius. Then all of them stood quiet for a moment, taking one another's measure.

"We thank y'all, Ruth and me do," Julius said, finally breaking the silence. "Wish we could repay such a blessing." He smiled and held out his hand toward Hamp.

Hamp hesitated. Were there rules in the outlands about shaking hands with Negras? Ma and Pap had rules on being polite. But he couldn't see Tate shaking hands with a Negra, even if they offered first. Before he could guess what to do, Julius curled his fingers into a fist and pulled his hand back. The smile on his face hardened into a blunt, unforgiving glare.

"We ought to be gettin'," Ruth said quickly. She lifted Mercy up higher on her hip and patted her back just like

Ma did L.B. Mercy yawned and buried her face in the crook of her mama's neck.

Neeta held out the haversack. "Here's you a few taters and a little bag of cornmeal and a tin can for boiling mush. Keep Mercy up on your shoulders and away from the gators. Careful of snakes, too."

"Bless you," Julius said, taking the sack. "You's got do-right in you, Miss Neeta. Makes me hopeful. God's hand is working in its mysterious ways, just like ol' preacher used to say."

"Amen," Ruth agreed. "Our prayers'll be answered, by 'm by." She pushed Mercy up on Julius's broad shoulders. Silver glossed the smooth planes of the little girl's cheeks and bare arms, and she hugged her papa's neck and rested her face on his matted thatch of hair. She stared at Hamp, her dark eyes wide and shiny as two moon-dazzled puddles.

He felt like she could see right inside his head, and so he looked away, out into gauzy wood. And to hear Julius and Ruth talk of prayers frabbled his thinking even more. What happened if God had to choose between two prayers that worked against each other? How could God decide between them?

He chewed his lip and tried to ignore Mercy's steady gaze. His main prayer was for the South to win the war, and he wished it more since Pap came home. How he hoped God would answer his prayer! But Julius probably figured Hamp wanted the South to win just so they'd

Kim L. Siegelson

have to keep slaving. Fact was, he'd not ever had thought one about slaves. Never worried over them one way or the other. Knew only that if the Yanks won, it'd be a bitter tonic to swallow.

It'd mean Pap give up his leg for nothing. It'd mean he give up Pap for nothing.

He didn't want to think no more, for it scoured his heart raw to do it. He needed to fix his mind on tracking down Duff and collecting bounty on him. He wondered how much Julius was worth. Not as much maybe, but something, and they were stealing it from Scrub. Made them no better than raiders—Yank or Reb.

Tight-jawed, he helped Julius set the smokehouse door straight in its frame, line up the hinge gudgeon and tamp the pintle into the socket so it held again. His heart skipped a thump when they rubbed hands. Julius's felt tough as boot leather, callused and strong and warm. Like Pap's. If he closed his eyes, he could imagine Pap's hands from that summer when they built the hunting camp on Rooter Island, their last one together.

He jammed his hand in his pocket and met Julius's eye, but couldn't hold it for long. Maybe helping this family would turn God's ear in a favorable direction next time he prayed, somehow put him in heaven's good graces. Show God it wasn't slaves but Yankees that deserved vengeance.

Besides, Julius and Ruth wasn't like Duff, a no-good murdering traitor who deserved to be caught and forced to swallow the same bitter justice he give his master. And by that measure, God might not count freeing these runaways as stealing. The idea eased him a little.

"If you've a mind, y'all can follow me through the swamp as far as Bugaboo Island," he said. "It's deep enough south that no one will bother you. If you know how to fish and trap, you can live all right for a while."

Neeta's mouth flew open, but for the first time Hamp could remember since she learned to talk, it took a long time for the words to squeeze past her teeth. "Let me fetch your gun, Hamp, so y'all can be off. I'll sneak back later to let Scrub's dogs out and brush the yard clean of footprints with a gallberry branch. Everything'll look regular as can be." She grinned and laughed out loud. "Oh, I wish I could be a bug on a branch, and see his face when he unlocks that smokehouse and opens the door!"

God and the dogs would likely be the only ones to take notice, Hamp figured, and they wasn't apt to tell the tale about how a family of Negras might've slipped through the wall chinks and vanished into the swamp without a trace. A secret between him and Neeta from now on. If she could keep it.

They all traveled together, backtracking along the path toward home. Hamp walked at the head carrying a lit pine-knot torch, more for comfort than for the light it threw out. When he reached a spot where another trail, scarcely more than a break in the brush, spurred off the wider path, he stopped and gave the torch to Neeta.

"You're halfway home. Stay to the trail. Don't get lost.

And keep your lips buttoned if Ma or Pap start asking questions."

"All right," she answered, tight-voiced. "But don't stay gone too long; be careful."

For a moment it seemed like she might clamp her arms around him, so Hamp nodded once, called out for Bone, and then turned south onto the new trail with Julius and Ruth at his heels. He glanced back over his shoulder and saw that the torch glow surrounded Neeta in a snug circle of light, a small golden room notched out of the fog and a-flitter with moths and lacewings. Barefooted and lank-legged, with the haversack slung over her shoulder, she looked to him like a spirit traveler—a fairy girl disguised as a wanderer. Then, eagerly, he plunged into the darkness that separated him from Duff.

Chapter 8

There was no easy traveling between Pinder and Bugaboo Island at night and on foot. Hamp ruled against lighting another pine-knot torch, for it'd draw every bug inside a half mile. And it'd take a hand none could spare to keep it held aloft.

"I'll stay to water as much as I can so Scrub's dogs

won't have an easy time of scenting your trail," he told Julius and Ruth so they wouldn't think he was trying to make the going hard for no good reason. He figured they'd have at least one day, maybe two for the trail to grow cold. At the same time he hoped Duff's trail would be easy to follow, once Bone caught wind of it. He hoped Duff kept to dry ground as much as he could.

But for them, it was mostly hard slogging through the channels, cypress bays and open prairies of water that matched the night sky in inky tint and seeming endlessness. On all sides unseen critters of great and small size called warning, splashed and scurried. Bone joined in it, dashing to and fro, plunging in and out, excited to be traveling.

The water wasn't more than ankle- to knee-deep, for the most part, but it was cold as January rain, and treacherous. Julius and Ruth stayed close, following without chat or sound excepting pulled breath and muttered prayer. Julius slipped or tripped many a time, but managed to catch himself each time and keep Mercy balanced atop his shoulders. Once Ruth stepped into a water-filled hole and sank past her waist in the muck. "Lord help us!" she cried out so loud, it sent a flock of sleeping egrets hurtling from their roost.

Sound traveled far over the water, more than a mile sometimes. Hamp prayed it hadn't reached all the way to Pinder. Or Duff, wherever he was.

Soon as Julius pulled Ruth free of the hole, she waded toward the shallows. Her wet skirt clung to her legs and made a slap-sucking sound with every step. She bent and braced herself, then reached down and took the skirt in a bunch and wrung water from it, hitched it up between her legs and tucked the back hem in at the front waistband so it looked like she wore baggy britches or nothing but pantaloons. Hamp shied from staring at her naked shins, gladful the darkness hid the red he felt creep into his face.

Finally, as the sky turned the silvery-rose of a sunfish's belly, the fog thinned to wisps and they caught sight of Bugaboo Island. Larger than most prairie heads and thicks, Bugaboo had a decent span of dry land a-bristle with a small stand of shade trees and loblolly, brushy with gallberry and huckleberry and hurrah bushes. Hamp knew of two wild beegums in hollow trees to the island's center, and there were plenty of frogs and fish to gig, birds and rabbits to trap, turtle eggs and turtles, too. Just a spit north of Rooter Island, but smaller by half, it was a good place for anyone wanting to hide. A family could stay put there for as long as they needed to, providing they knew how to live off the land.

He didn't know if Julius and Ruth could, but that wasn't his worry now. They'd be on their own like they'd set out to be.

"That there's Bugaboo," Hamp said, pointing it out to Julius. "You can make it from here without me. There's some honey trees to the center, if you can find 'em, food if you can catch it. You should be safe there for a while, but watch out for rattlers and cottonmouths. And keep

Mercy away from the water. She'd be less than a mouthful for some of the bigger gators in here."

Julius nodded. "We'll stay and rest a piece, then head out." He held up the haversack and said, "You and your sister is the only two I ever met to help us."

"Thank Neeta, not me," Hamp answered, too quick. He'd not meant his voice to sound so sour.

A tiny muscle twitched like a lizard's tail at the back of Julius's jaw, and Hamp felt his own jaw muscles tighten, too. After a pause that seemed thick as cold grits, he swung his pack to front and dug inside till he found the chunk of wrapped salt pork. He drew in a deep breath and said, "Go on and take this. It'll round out the meal and taters Neeta give you."

Julius hesitated until Ruth laid a hand on the back of his shoulder. Then he reached out only halfway so Hamp had to stretch a little farther to put the bundle in his hand.

"I best be going," Hamp mumbled. He whistled for Bone and turned his back on Julius and Ruth, got his bearings and headed south again, this time along the dry edge of Bugaboo. He felt them watch him for a time, but he didn't turn around to say fare-thee-well, nor did he raise his hand to wave. Whatever fate befell their family from now on, at least it'd be set by their hands and God's. No other.

Now he could fix his mind on picking up Duff's trail. Duff, a different kind of runaway: alone and desperate, crafty and mean. Six toes, too. He remembered a Sunday past when the preacher read from the Bible about six being the devil's own number and sign, just as three belonged to God. For five hundred in gold, though, he'd fight the devil himself on a bed of hot coals.

He said the words aloud, then shivered. A lump gathered in the hollow of his gut, a knot of cold, heavy fear. He adjusted the gun slung over his back, comforted by the solid weight of it pressed against his spine, and leapt to the closest dry spot he could reach. Looked around for gators before he jumped again. Bone splashed along behind him.

A tall, flinthead crane trumpeted *karrrooo* from its grassy mound of a nest and leapt into the air, its wings unfolding in such slow measure that they appeared to work by method of ropes and pulleys instead of muscle and bone. As it flapped higher into the brightening sky, Bone leapt after its trailing feet, snapping once before plunging into the water through a raft of floating bonnet lilies. His head broke the surface and he paddled to Hamp with a lily leaf for a cap.

"Careful, boy, you know how gators love the taste of a dog!" Hamp railed at him. Daggit, if he didn't sound like Ma. But if anything happened to Bone . . . Just the thought of losing Bone wrenched his innards, made him want to snatch Bone up and keep him safe.

Bone scrambled out and shook the water off his pelt. He lowered his rump end onto a clump of grass and gave

Hamp a tongue-lolling dog grin. Hamp smiled back, trying to let go the worry. Worry did no good, and Bone was safe as he'd ever been.

He ruffled Bone's ears and took a deep pull of air until he felt his chest expand to aching, then blew out with a sharp cry, "Karrrooo!" It matched exactly the voice of the crane. Sometimes it was hard to breathe on Pinder Island. Almost like Pap and Ma and Neeta and even L.B. took more than their share of the air, with only a little bit left for him. Out in the swamp he didn't have to share with anyone but Bone, and Bone didn't ask for much.

The little tussock of land they rested on felt springy and wobbly under Hamp's feet, like a great floating flapjack. He jumped up and down on it and whooped like a wild thing, like a great gray-feathered crane. It shook beneath him until the myrtle bushes that grew at the center began to quiver. Bone splayed his legs wide to keep his balance on the bobbing land, and cocked his head sideways.

Hamp held the musket up to his eye and took aim at a myrtle bush on another tussock, a specter in the thinning mist. "Got you sighted, Duff," he whispered. "No mercy."

Before he got an imaginary shot off, his legs broke through the tussock floor and plunged him hip-deep into the swamp. He pushed up quick onto a solid spot and looked down into the hole he'd made. An orange spider he'd knocked down skated across the little lake. Quick as spit, a jackfish tipped itself faceup and snatched the spider under and disappeared. The dark surface rippled briefly, and then grew still and glassy, and Hamp stared down at his own face staring up, captured inside the gape.

He frabbled the water with his fingers and crawled backward to more solid ground to check his gear. The wooden musket stock had taken a quick dunking, but the muzzle, pointed skyward, was dry. Lucky. Pap might skin him alive if the musket got drowned, or lost. Then he'd have to make do in the swamp forever, hiding from Pap like a runaway, living like the Indians back in the olden days before settlers came.

'Twas the Indians who first put a name to the swamp, Pap said. Okefenokee, they called it—trembling earth. And he said the tussock islands bobbed like they did because they'd not latched on to the swamp bottom yet.

"The island roots go to winding down through that dark water, and the swamp bottom builds up till they can touch just the littlest bit," Pap had said, dangling the fingers of one hand down at the straight-up fingers of the other. "Well, sir, they might take ahold and grow together solid, or they might break away and have to start over again." He wove the fingers of both hands together for a moment, then yanked them apart.

"Might take a hundred or even a thousand years of starting over and over, but they keep at it. Keep on reaching."

Hamp pinched the white button top off a hatpin flower and rolled it between his palms. He missed listening to Pap talk about the swamp and everything else: all the secret hunting and fishing and trapping spots; the way to find direction using bird flight and shadows and stars; how to blaze a trail so you could find it again; plants that might heal what ailed you and them that were food.

Ma knew book learning, and she taught Neeta and him reading and numbers and such, but Pap knew swamp lore and stories from all the way back to Gre-gre-granpap. But Pap had passed just part of it on before the war, and nothing since.

Pap was cheating him out of something that belonged to him by right, was stealing from him, and it wasn't fair. Wasn't a thing Hamp could ever forgive.

He stood and pitched the hatpin bloom into the hole, its water no longer dark but red as the eye of a blue-beaked heron. The flower spun and bobbled over the reflected sunrise, a tiny pale island afloat on a fiery pond.

C h a p t e r   9

He and Bone traveled on through morning. The fog burned away with the sun's rise, but the memory of it lingered in the air, moist and heavy. The warmth drew sweat beads to Hamp's brow and neck, and dampened his shirt collar and his back beneath the gun

Kim L. Siegelson

and pack. And warmth drew out a multitude of gators and snakes and turtles, each willing to fight for claim over whatever little sunny spot could be found. Be it a patch of grass, a loblolly limb, or a cypress stump, some scaly critter basked atop it, beady eyes watchful, ready to battle.

"Pea-brained lizards!" Hamp yelled at two bull gators bellowing at each other over a soggy mud wallow. They hissed and brayed and rumbled, and paid no heed to any voice but their own.

A few times he took from his shirt pocket the strip of torn cloth left in the shed by Duff so Bone could sniff it. Each time Bone raised up to scent the air and then bent to snuffle the dirt before he pushed south again, staying mostly to dry land.

When they reached Rooter Island, middle day was long past and shadows trailed at Hamp's heels. Rooter wasn't much different from Bugaboo, other than being smaller, but still firm along the banks, with thicks toward the center, shady hummocks of pine and water oak and gumball trees. Soon as his feet touched it, Hamp knew it to be his sunny spot in the swamp, the ground he'd fight for if he was a bull gator. The one place he went to when Pap was gone that he felt close to him. Still did.

Maybe it had a Indian name like the swamp did, but Pap named it Rooter after the wild bristle-back hogs called piney woods rooters. The skull of one hung over the mantel shelf at Scrub's place. Heavy and big as the blade of a push plow, the head's empty eye holes, long snout and two curved tusks sprouted from lower jaw put in mind demon images of the kind Ma said was waiting for folks in Satan's realm.

Rooters ate anything: pine tree roots, huckleberries, acorns, even meat. Pap said he'd seen a passel of especially big ones bring down a bear. "One by one they run in, a-lashing its legs with tusk and hooves till it fell down bawling. Then they rushed on it like a mob of squealing devils and finished it while I watched from up in a tree. Curdle your blood and stop your heart to bear witness." Between the gators and bears and swampers, Pap promised all the rooters had been hunted off the island, for there'd not been sign of them in long years.

'Twas likely still so, but all the same Hamp kept eyes open for hog tracks and droppings, and scraped-out furrows and wallows.

The marshy shore firmed and turned sandy along the inland trail toward the hunting camp. Dense brush thinned to scrub and wiregrass and palmetto. Gray squirrels scurried up the trunks of trees and heckled them, and all varieties of bird life twittered and flittered amongst the upper branches. But Bone didn't give chase. He hung close now, serious, his dog sense tuned to tracking and hunting—the work of Rooter Island. Trotting a few steps ahead, he sometimes stopped to lift nose to air and sniff deep. Hamp smelled pinesap, and mushrooms, and something else faintly sweet and blooming, but knew Bone scented a more powerful mix: of plant and animal, of old and new, of what belonged and what didn't.

He slipped his hand inside the pocket of his shirt and

fingered the strip of cloth torn from Duff's clothes. Duff didn't belong. Did Bone sense him somewhere close by now? Duff wouldn't dare to show himself if he was. Scrub and Tate had agreed on one thing: Negras was cowardly as a rule, and quick to run from trouble. Made them poor soldier material, and highlighted a prime reason Abe Lincoln shouldn't free them like he wanted. Negras would be doomed without a master to take care of them, for it'd be like turning children out into the wild.

Maybe that was right, Hamp thought. What if they'd done more wrong than good in letting Julius and Ruth and Mercy go free? The swamp didn't forgive mistakes or ignorance.

He checked the traps he'd set off the trail some days before, hoping to find supper. His belly felt hollow as a pitcher gourd, and he wondered what fool notion had pushed him into giving away his only sure meal.

Two loop snares he found empty and unsprung. He scattered a new layer of leaf litter over them. Something had raided two of his spring traps and left one with remnants of brown fur at the edges. Probably a bear or a wildcat had come upon whatever he'd trapped and taken it. The last of the traps was nothing but a weighted basket set up in a strip of sand scrub close to the camp. He could see it was tripped before he got close. It lay rim down and of a whole piece, and whatever critter it held inside lay quiet. Bone charged it, but stopped short and shied away as the rise and fall rattling of a cane viper warned him off.

Through the basket chinks Hamp saw the coils pull in

tight and the flattened head waver from side to side, working a bead on Bone. Growling and wary, Bone crept closer, his neck slung down between his shoulders. With each step the rattling grew louder, gathering strength till it sounded like a forest of storm-shivered leaves. Then, in a blink, the basket jerked forward and up with the sudden force of the viper's strike.

Bone leapt skyward, spun round in midair, and hit the dirt with all paws scrabbling. The basket popped forward again and this time flipped sideways. Bone rushed at Hamp, cut to and fro across the path between him and the snake, yanked his britches legs so he tumbled backward, and then took him by the shirt collar. The rattler lifted up tall as a pipe weed and shook its tail buttons. When neither Hamp nor Bone made a move toward it, it seemed to realize it'd come out the winner and let the shivering racket taper off to a clatter. Satisfied, it sank down and slithered into the palmetto thick.

"Daggit! You can stop tearing at me now it's gone." Hamp sat up and rubbed his neck. "Snake hain't a bad meal, when you're hungry. I didn't need you to save me."

Bone sagged against him and drummed his tail on the ground, his eyes on the spot where the viper had disappeared.

The trail opened into a egg-shaped clearing not far from a channel of a small lake called Duck Pond. A raised platform of hewn cypress logs marked the center of the clearing, the platform he and Pap had built. He dropped his pack and other trumpery onto the planks, spangled with bird spatters and strewn with seed hulls and leaves. A rack of deer antlers hung on the side of a gumball tree beside the platform, and he rested the musket and shot bag on it. The antlers had come from the first deer he took on his own at age nine.

Back then his arms barely had strength enough to hold steady the weight of the musket—to his thinking, something akin to balancing a house pole on an even plane. It was more than pure heft that set him to shaking. He'd been seized with the idea that he couldn't do what Pap had taught him; he'd stall too long, or miss, or wound the deer and not kill it right off.

But then Pap's whiskery cheek had drawn up against his, and Pap's chest pressed in warm and hard as a timber wall against his back. He still pictured Pap's hands, sun brown and strong, helping to steady him so he could aim true. "You'll know when you're ready," he'd whispered when the buck wandered in range. "Take your time." Even muffled, his voice sounded deep and certain as a river current back then.

He'd kept up the hunting camp so it'd be ready when Pap came home, but he was good as gone now, dried up like a pond in summer without rain. Time run out. Pap'd never see what he'd learned on his own. How steady his arms held the musket now, and how true his aim.

It didn't matter anymore. He ran his hand down Bone's back and let it stay there. "At least I got you, old boy. We don't need Pap. The two of us can catch that boy without him."

He wished to sit awhile and let himself drift backward in memory, but restless hunger jabbed him. With his folding knife he whittled a double-pronged stick to sharp points. Along the water's edge of a narrow, weed-choked channel he soon gigged a mess of ten yam-sized bullfrogs. Overhead the sky dimmed and the air cooled till it pulled mist up from the swamp, vapor that hung over the water like a mourning veil.

At camp he piled wood into the fire circle beside the platform and kindled a flame with a flint and steel. His belly gnawed on itself while he waited for it to burn down to cooking coals, while he separated the frog legs from each stumpy body. Finally, nearly faint with hunger, he speared batches of the skinned legs onto the fork end of the gig and roasted them until they sputtered juice and turned brown. He ate with doglike purpose and concentration, barely chewing, sucking the bones clean as peeled twigs.

When he'd eaten all, he wiped his mouth on his forearm and lay back with his blanket under his head to study the star patterns. A lone mosquito whined near his ear, and he swiped at it. Moths and lacewings dove at the fire, only to spiral back up as bright sparks that sputtered out like tiny shooting stars. Beyond the platform, darkness pressed sooty walls against the fire's light. Peeper frogs struck up a high-pitched chorus, less akin to singing than the noise made by a stick drawn over a washboard. The voices of what bullfrogs had been spared joined in the calaberment.

Bone hitched himself up of a sudden, and grew taut-limbed and prick-eared. Hamp put his hand out to ease him, and felt a low growl rumble beneath his fingers. He tried to see what Bone could. Scanned the shadowy fan palms that surrounded the platform, but could see nothing beyond the small circle of light thrown out by the fire. His scalp prickled with dread. Two pictures came to mind in double flashes: the phantom bear from his nightmare, and a dark, faceless boy clutching a knife in his fist. The frog legs kicked in his gut like they wanted to swim back upstream.

A tree shook nearby and a voice shrieked like a shoat caught in a gator's jaws. *"Skeeeee!"*

A shadow passed over their heads and troubled the air, and Hamp threw back his head, relieved. "Daggit, Bone! You like to scared the daylights out of me! That's just a old scritch owl hunting his dinner."

But then some said a scritch owl could bring bad luck unless you charmed it away. Bad luck was about the only thing he didn't need another portion of, so he hooked his pointer fingers together and yanked them hard as a ward against it.

He sat wide-eyed, stroking Bone's neck to ease him. But Bone stayed hunkered down, tight as the latch on a firing pin, and stared without blinking at the heavy gray mist that hung over the lake. His chest rumbled against the platform.

For just a moment a breeze stirred it. Was there a flicker of light far beyond the trees on the other side of

Duck Pond? Sparks above the trees, or a swarm of fire-flies? When Hamp tried to focus on it, the foggy curtain drew closed again. Made him feel afeared and chary.

He hedged to the tree and took the musket from the antler rack, and then lay down with it next to Bone. Cradled the gun to him the way Neeta held to her moss doll at night. The way Ma sometimes held Pap.

Chapter 10

Morning broke cool and gray-tinged as gosling down. Hamp woke damp with dew. The sun still hung low in its slot to the east. The musket rested at a tilt across his thighs, and Bone at his feet. He yawned and worked the kinks from his neck while Bone stretched with front paws out, rump high.

Shiverish, Hamp held his hand over the mound of ash in the fire pit until he found a warm spot where a coal still smoldered, then blew it to new life and added kindling.

Holding close to the warmth, he loosed the tie on the shot bag and poured the lead slugs on his blanket. Counted six—a piddling small cluster of grape. Pap had two lead bars set by as makings for new shot, but he'd clearly not got round to casting. At least the powder horn was nearly full, and he had cotton wadding aplenty. Hamp scooped the balls into his hand and poured them back in the bag. He'd have to be stingy and careful, as if they were nuggets of pure silver.

His stomach gurgled as reminder he'd given it but one paltry meal of roasted frog swimmers since leaving Pinder Island. Bone noozled and pawed at the pack, likely scenting the chunk of salt pork that wasn't there. "Got to fish for our breakfast," Hamp reminded him. "Once our hollows is full, we'll go Duff hunting."

His own voice stopped him cold. "Duff hunting," he whispered. Sounded like nothing, akin to duck hunting. Easy as spitting melon seeds. But his chest seized up at the thought of the boy, of what he might have to do if he found him. He'd only ever aimed a gun at wild animals, didn't know if he could shoot another person.

Pap knew what it was like to shoot a living, breathing person. Hamp figured he'd put lead slugs into nearly every variety of Yankee man on the battlefield, for he'd listened in secret once when Scrub asked Pap to tell him about the warring. He'd never heard Pap speak of it before or since.

His voice was husky low, every word pinched. Of Shiloh he said, " 'Bout fearful as you'd expect, and strange as a dream. We laid up in a orchard of peach trees abloom in pink and white, as peaceful a place as I've seen to this day. Then something akin to thunder boomed and the trees shivered petals a-loose so it seemed a snow flurry had come up. 'Twasn't thunder but big carriage guns launching shells. They come screaming at us, woo-ooo-oo pow! Lot of times they goes astray and hits the trees and sends splinters and flowers and metal bits flying all directions. Might sheer off a treetop. I seen big ones with girth wide and stout as brick chimneys snap like little broom straws and catch afire. I seen men crushed, get trapped and burned under such.

"Well, sir, gunners will find your range sooner or later and hit true, then it's blood-sticky mud, rocks, scraps of horse and men that lands all about, heavy as hail out of the sky. Once they find range, you can't stay put, got to up and charge or get blown to parts. And round about then is when the air thickens with flying lead, akin in sound and fury to a plague of black hornets. Seemed like if you held your hat up, why, it'd be like filling a sack with a corn funnel."

He hesitated and Hamp could hear the scratchy, hissing sound of his hand kneading the blunt end of his thigh. "Boys all around go to yelling, running, falling, and every face like the others—stained blue-black with powder spray so's eye whites and teeth take on a glowy, demon look. Things get so mixed up, it's hard to say if you've fired on friend or foe. And the air turns powerful foul with sulphur smoke, sour tree sap, churned dirt and stink of busted horse gut and men. Every breath sets you a-retching and your eyes to watering up so as all in your vision is fuzzed. A blessing. The blur helps you believe the happenings to be a figment untrue, a nightmare to wake from at mornglowm."

Scrub whistled through his teeth, but offered no comment.

"But then you do wake," Pap went on. "To a feast for maggots and blowflies. Clots of buzzards and black crows flock like undertakers round a banquet table."

At that, both fell silent, and out of chat.

Hamp could picture Pap in battle with ball whizzing past on all sides, could see him aim and fire his gun like he'd done hundreds of times in the swamp. But when he pictured the Yankees Pap fired on, he couldn't imagine faces, only uniform coats and britches and boots. They fell over like scarecrows: no blood, no sounds, nothing moved. Crack! Thud. Crack! Thud. Like sacks of cornmeal shot off a fence rail.

But when he let himself see Pap get hit, it was different. Like a shot deer, his legs crumpled under like they'd suddenly turned to water, his arms flew out to catch himself. He had a face, and it looked surprised, then tight-lipped against the pain, like when he slipped off the roof once and hurt himself. Pap was brave against fear and honorable. Unlike Duff, who'd used battle as cover to do murder.

Hamp swallowed the stone lodged in his throat. If it came to shooting, he'd hold that in his mind. He'd yank the trigger hard and fast. But he'd try not to kill Duff. Maybe just wound him, then haul him to camp, tie him up to the gumball tree and go fetch help. Let Tate do the killing.

Once he found Duff, it'd be simple. Pap went up against a thousand Yankee soldiers. Even Neeta could take on one darkie boy who'd lived most his life as spoiled companion to a rich outlander. Ought not take long to capture him, if he hadn't already got himself drowned or snakebit or gator-snatched.

First, he had to rid himself of hunger.

He took the char-pointed gig in hand and called Bone. A bull gator bellowed as they drew close to Duck Pond Lake. There the swamp prairie stretched out wide. A sheet of honey-tinted water rippled away from them toward another bit of land within swimming distance. Narrow channels of water cut through the prairie, bordered by wide mats of bonnet lilies and spiky never-wets whose flowers looked for all the world like a slender version of a crane's head. Pap called it the Duck Pond because the open water always teemed with a mixed crowd of wood ducks, mallards, ringnecks and ruddies. They paddled and preened in groups, the males circling the females and flapping at each other.

Bone quivered at the sight of the birds but stayed quiet the way Pap had trained him so he'd not spook them. Hamp crouched down beside him to watch them, wishing he had just one shot to waste. He craved a mouthful of oily duck meat and fire-crisped skin, a drumstick big enough to hold in his fist. Maybe he could call one close enough to gig like a frog. Holding his hands

Kim L. Siegelson

prayer style, he covered his mouth and pinched his nose tight with fingertips, then pushed out a bleating quack through open palms. A green-headed mallard tipped his head toward the sound, curious.

Then the myrtle bushes that fringed the island across the water caught Hamp's eye before he let out a second call. Rustling movement. Some big animal. He hunkered lower in the weeds, expecting deer or bear to come out and take a drink. His breath left him in a rush. A boy stepped from the bay brush and stood still and wary as any wild critter in the swamp.

He stripped off his raggedy britches and shirt and hung them from a twig. Naked as a newborn, his body from forehead to ankles the warm brown color of blackstrap molasses, he waited a moment before quickly sliding himself into the shallow lake. He let the inky water cover all but his face, which matched in hue so nearly that he was close to invisible. With slow movements he gathered lily pad leaves and flowers in a bunch and circled them close to his cheeks and chin. Once hidden inside the wreath of lilies, the boy glided across the water, making barely a ripple as Hamp watched. A group of female mallards took no notice as he drew close to them.

Bone whined and Hamp clamped his hand over his muzzle. In the time it took to do so, a brown duck jerked feet first beneath the water, same as if a snapping turtle had snatched it under. Only a few bubbles floated where it had been. The rest of the mallards scooted away from the spot in a flurry.

Hamp sat in wonderment as the boy returned to the bank and drew his lanky body from the water. There he stood, the sun shining off his wet skin and the feet of the drowned duck clutched in his hand. He shook his head so water sprayed from it, then gathered his clothes into his arms and pushed back through the brush, whistling a tune.

"Dag, that was slick as a frog's back," Hamp whispered. "Tricky-smart as anything I ever seen." Bone tipped his head up and whined again, his tongue curling up to slick back the whiskers on his muzzle. His tail swished an arc in the dirt around his rump.

Hamp studied the opposite shore, his hunger suddenly forgotten. The boy could be no other but Duff. Daggit! If he'd just brought the musket with him, he could've captured the boy without much struggle. Maybe if he and Bone moved quick, they could still catch him by surprise.

He tossed the gig aside and hoofed it back to camp for the musket and shot. His stomach felt as knotted up as a gob of fishing worms as he checked the musket, loaded it, rechecked it. Before he could talk himself out of it, he retraced his path to the lake. There he peeled his clothes off and laid them on the ground. Rolled his rifle and shot bag up in them and held the bundle over his head as he waded into the water, determined, but with heart yammering. The way he pictured Pap, charging toward the enemy lines at Shiloh. All life seemed whittled down to one fine point: right against wrong, swamper against outlander, one color against another.

Bone plunged in behind him with a great splash. The ducks scooted away as they cut across, the large flock splitting in half to let them through. Bone lunged toward the group on the right, and it rose up from the water in a wild, honking whirlwind. Waves slapped against Hamp's chest, rippling out bigger and bigger in rings that lapped against the land, both forward and behind.

Chapter 11

Hamp pulled himself up on the opposite shore where the boy had been and goosebumped in the breeze. While he pulled his shirt and britches on, Bone flapped himself dry and snuffled along the muddy ground, stopping to sneeze water he'd sucked up his snout. He reached a gap in the brush and tested every inch of the ground, licked it, and took to sniffing anew.

"What'd you find, Bone?" Hamp whispered. He stooped down and pondered the boy's prints pressed in the mud, perfect six-toed matches for those left in the shed and smokehouse on Pinder. He traced them with his trigger finger, stood and checked his rifle to make sure it was dry and ready, then checked again to be safe. He could feel the air buzz with Bone's impatience at him.

Hamp finally released him with a sharp spoken order: "Go, dog, course 'em!"

Bone snorted the spongy dirt one last time—deep-breathed in and out—then shot through the brush like a pig after persimmons. Hamp followed behind as close as he could. Twigs and spiky gumballs jabbed his bare feet, but the pads were tough as boot leather and didn't pain him like the cat's claw and greenbrier that tore at his arms, or the little teeth of saw palmetto that snagged on his britches legs. There wasn't a cleared trail, nor even a deer path to follow like on Pinder or Rooter, and he'd cursed himself for forgetting to bring a hack blade along.

Bone, with his short, slick pelt, slipped through the tangle easy as a needle through a hemp sack. Hamp listened to him course along ahead and wished he'd be quieter. If Duff heard him, he'd sure enough hide, or turn tail and run.

Hamp wrestled his way through a thick stand of myrtle bushes and stumbled into a clearing no bigger than their cabin at Pinder, edged by sapling trees and heavy brush. From the looks of it, he'd found Duff's camp, but the suddenness and the openness of it made him feel as addled and uneasy as one of Tate's grayback racers. Tense and wild-eyed, he raised the musket to his shoulder and spun around, aiming it everywhere, the prick of eyes always on his back, no matter what direction he turned.

He stopped and listened, mouth breathing like he'd been hard running. Heard nothing but swamp sound.

"Daggit," Hamp muttered under his breath, half

relieved and half piked Duff was gone. And gone quick, for it appeared he'd left everything behind.

A peeled log had been dragged close to a small fire pit. A gunnysack rolled into a sort of pillow padded the top of the log, and a dented tin can and flint box rested beside the pad. In the dirt to the front lay a limp, half-plucked duck. Pale, speckled feathers tumbled across the clearing like dried flower petals and snagged in the low branches of the myrtles so the bushes looked fuzzy about the ankles.

He picked up the gunnysack and unfurled it with a snap. The smell of cornmeal and smoke whiffed up, and something dropped from inside it to the ground. Hamp squatted down and plucked up a bundle of different bird feathers tied in a bunch with a piece of string. Feathers of redbird, jackdaw, scoot, turkey gobbler, swamp owl, pink curlew, and some he didn't know. He dropped them and picked up a whistle carved from a finger-thick section of twig. A tiny, perfect bird with open beak perched at the end opposite the mouthpiece, its body whittled into form from a burl or offshoot. Hamp rolled it between his fingers, admiring it. A fanciful, unexpected thing to find. Something Neeta would like. He pushed it into his pocket and bent closer to study the footprints pressed in the dirt to the front of the log.

The image of the splay-toed print was his last thought before he heard the crack and felt a sudden burst of pain at the back of his skull. Brilliant light pulsed behind his eyelids like chain lightning. Iron bells clanged in his ears.

He did not turn, nor see who'd clubbed him, before his face hit the ground. He knew only blank and dreamless nothing.

• • •

He roused with Bone licking his cheek. A drum thumped inside his brainpan, and his eyes seemed not able to hold on a steady bead or clear picture. His head felt damp and sticky, as if somebody'd doused it with syrup. He reached back of it for a feel, and discovered a raised knot on his scalp big as a goose egg. Drew his fingers back bloody.

"Just set still," a deep voice warned. "Got your gun aimed straight at your gut."

Hamp sat quiet, unmoving, letting the lint clear from his head. It seemed to drain from his head to his throat and lodge there. He tried to swallow the lump, but could gather no wet from his mouth. "Just out hunting with my dog," he croaked, embarrassed at how his voice came out wobbly and breathless, at how his knees trembled inside the wide legs of his britches. And he needed to let go his water something fierce, but he'd die before he asked permission from some murdering darkie. He'd pee himself first.

"Seems like a lot of islands in this swamp to choose from. Funny how you ended up here in my little bitty camp."

Hamp turned his head enough to look slantwise at the boy. His shirt resembled a collection of dirty ribbons

Kim L. Siegelson

draped over his chest, kindred to the strip Hamp had found in the shed. Raggedy, kneeless butternut britches hung off bony hips and legs with less meat on them than a chair frame. He wore a gray hat so flabby, it appeared melted to his head, the brim of it half hiding his face. Pap's heavy musket balanced in his hands with ease.

Hamp glanced down at his feet and counted his toes. "I know about you," he said. "You stole some bacon from our smokehouse. Hain't that right?"

The boy's face beneath the hat brim crumpled into a frown. He slid down on the log and pulled his feet up, but kept the musket level. "Ain't stole nothing," he snapped. "A lady come out to hush the dogs, and spied me hiding in the corncrib. She pointed me the path here and give me some bacon 'fore I left."

"Liar!" Hamp blurted.

Duff snorted a half laugh, but didn't argue. A yellow fly landed on the thick of his arm and probed for a second before he swatted it and flicked it into the dirt. A red bead of blood gathered up from the place where it'd bit him, and he smeared it into a rusty line with his palm, licked it without thinking. The duck, now fully plucked, roasted beside a fire on a spike whittled out of green wood. Greasy drippings sputtered and popped and sent up flares of flame that charred the duck's skin.

"If Ma give you that bacon, she oughtn't have. You don't deserve it." He stopped himself from saying more.

The boy worked his mouth into a knot and then out

again, but his face softened a bit. "Maybe I don't deserve kindness, but maybe I do. Can't nobody judge me but God. That's what the Lord's book say, for true."

He let go the musket to pull a knife from his waistband, and poked it into the duck's thigh. Clear juice trickled from it and sputtered in the heat below. He pulled the leg away from the duck's carcass, sliced through the joint, and held it out toward Hamp. "Hungry?"

The sight sent Hamp's stomach to rumbling and reminded him that he hadn't eaten for a long time. Felt like his stomach had sunk back against his backbone, but there was a queasy edge to his hunger, a sourness at his pit.

When he didn't take the drumstick, Duff shrugged and took a huge bite. Grease smeared his mouth and chin. He slurped juice and smacked his lips when he chewed. Finished, he tossed the bones to the side. Hamp glared at Bone, who raced to snatch them up. His tail wagged with joy as he cracked them between his teeth.

Turncoat traitor! Hamp thought. He couldn't sit anymore, just waiting. More than gold, all he wanted now was to get away. Go back to Pinder. He felt inside his pocket for his folding knife, the only weapon he had left, but found nothing there except the whistle he'd taken. Then he remembered, he'd put the knife aside after cleaning the frogs, and not picked it up again.

Duff yanked off the second drumstick and gnawed it. The musket rested across his thighs. Hamp measured the distance between them, and Duff's size to his. The boy was a good bit taller, but skinny. Maybe he could lunge out and topple him off the log. Use the surprise to grapple the musket away, for he'd almost as soon be shot than go home with empty hands, with less than he started out with.

He took a deep breath and started to his feet. Darkness flooded in, and heaviness, like a cowhide had been thrown atop him. He slumped back onto his hams, dizzy and pukeish. "What'll you do with me?" he asked after he'd caught his breath and the quell of sickness had ebbed from him.

Duff put his hand on the musket. "You lived here all your life?"

"I'm a pure swamper," Hamp answered. He wanted to add, *Just like my pap, who'll be coming to find me if I don't get home soon.*

He wished it were so.

Duff folded his hat brim up and studied him. Rolled his bottom lip in, bit a tag of skin off and chewed on it. "Well, swamper, I'll wager you know the quickest way to Florida."

Hamp knew how to get there. Pap had explained it once. But he'd never gone south that deep, hadn't a need for it. He remembered Pap saying it was twenty or thirty miles across Grand Prairie, and when you came upon the St. Mary's River, you could follow it into Florida. Two or three days' travel by punt boat, a lot more hoofing it over land and water. He could only guess.

Duff laughed once and shook his head in wonderment. "I needed me a guide, and here one is, delivered right to me." He smiled and gestured at Hamp with the duck's leg. "Looks like you going to Florida, swamper."

Hamp's mind raced in ten directions. Florida?! No! Too far. And he didn't know the trails, the switchbacks. Pap hadn't taken him farther than where they were sitting. He mightn't get home ever again. A new bout of dizziness rocked him.

He didn't want to leave Ma and Neeta wondering what had happened to him. Ma standing out on the porch at mornglowm and at evening, just waiting and waiting the way she'd done before Pap came home. Only this time there'd be a day she'd know to give up, and she'd not watch for him again.

What would Pap do? he wondered, and felt choked. Stricken. Why hadn't he tried harder to fix things? Now it was too late.

Or not. Maybe he could reason with Duff. He strained to keep his voice tethered. "In Florida they got slave catchers thicker than fleas on a dog's neck. You ought to be running northways, toward all them abolitionists wanting you. Toward the Yankees."

"Somebody down in Florida I got to find," Duff answered.

Hamp threw a doubtful look in his direction.

"It's true!" Duff insisted, puffing up with indignation. "Massa sold my sister, Sumi, to a sugar farmer last year, and I aim to find her. I promised Mama if I got free, that's what I'd do: go find Sumi, first thing."

But you murdered to get your freedom! Hamp wanted to shout. You shot a boy who couldn't defend himself. He smiled to remember Lieutenant Angus Tate's promise to his brother Gavin: kill Duff, first thing.

"You think it's something to smile at?" Duff asked, barely controlling the rise in his voice. "Well, it ain't. My mama ain't smiled a day since Sumi left us. Broke her heart. Especially since Massa swore up and down he'd never let a one of our family be sold. Said he had blood family he favored less."

He gave Hamp a withering glare and added, "I always knew you couldn't trust nothing a buchra promised. But I wanted to believe it. Like Mama did."

Hamp met Duff's glare with one of his own. "Must've had a good reason to get rid of her."

"You think so?" Duff answered, mocking. "They sold my sister on account of Massa's oldest son, Angus Tate. He wouldn't let her be, scared her with his lurking and pawing when she worked in the house. So Sumi went to Mistus about it, hoping something might be done to keep him away. Well, sir, what they done was sell her." He let a cold smile linger on his face for a moment before he continued.

"Can't trust a buchra no farther than you can throw him. That's why I ain't waiting for no Yankee buchras to keep their promises or give me freedom. I seen what they're handing out to colored who join 'em, and it ain't a lick different from being Massa's boy. Nawsir, them Yanks ain't no friend of mine." He tossed the half-eaten duck leg to Bone and wiped his fingers on the gunnysack pad. "I don't need no friends. What I need is for you to show me Florida so I can find Sumi. I like to keep my promises."

"Well, least we agree on Yankees," Hamp muttered. "But maybe you oughtn't trust me, feeling as you do." Soon as the words left his mouth, he knew it was so. He could guide Duff wrong. Take him in a big circle, lose him somewhere, lead him to danger.

Duff's face looked as smooth and untroubled as a wooden mask. "Never said I trusted you, swamper. But I think both of us knows a swamp like this ain't friendly to ones who don't really know it. So unless there's a colored swamper nearby, I got no choice but you—and you got no choice, either." He sawed a hunk from the duck's breast and held it out toward Hamp on the point of the blade. "You best fill up before we leave, 'cause there's no saying when we'll get another meal."

Hamp took the piece of meat in pinchered fingers. He bit into the warm, plum-colored flesh and chewed. Hungry as he'd been earlier, he wasn't anymore. The first oily swallow gagged him, then threatened to come back up. He closed his eyes and tore off another bite. Chewed it to pulp to make the swallowing easier. Bone slid to the ground beside him and waited for a scrap.

Hamp realized Duff hadn't told his name yet. He couldn't use it till it was told him or Duff would figure he knew more than he'd let on, and it'd not been ducks he'd

Kim L. Siegelson

been hunting after all. Already certain of the answer, he asked, "You got a name?"

Duff looked out into the trees, worked his mouth for a second and said, "Call me Gavin."

Gavin?! Hamp glowered, lost for all words but one: *liar*. Taking the name of a boy he'd murdered! The gall of it turned Hamp's stomach. He tossed the rest of his duck meat at Bone and scrubbed his fingers in the dirt. Slowly, thoughtfully he repeated the name Duff called himself. "Gavin . . . I used to know a boy of that same name. A hero killed in the war. Not a'tall like you."

"Lot of boys killed in the war," Duff answered in a similar thoughtful tone. "Least one or two of every name anybody ever thought up. Some of them names a thousand times dead. What's yours?"

"Hamp," he answered. "My dog's Bone."

The corners of Duff's lips pushed into a smile that seemed more grimace, like he'd got a taste of vinegar in his mouth. "Hamp," he said. "Yes, seems I do recollect a soldier boy with your name. Shot through the back. Died a coward, running from the fighting."

Hamp scowled at Duff with all the anger he could muster behind his eyes. Heat colored his face; he could feel it burn in his cheeks. Daggit! How he hated to know Duff could see it rise up in him.

Duff grinned like a carved pumpkin, but this time his teeth showed and his eyes crimped at the corners. "Don't you swampers know how to take a jest?"

Hamp refused to answer. Duff shrugged, pushed the duck meat into his own mouth and chewed, triumphant.

Chapter 12

If something goes wrong, don't let panic addle you, Hamp. Clear-headed thinking is your best tool, and don't hesitate to change course when your gut says you ought to. Hamp tried to keep his mind clutched round those words. He remembered Pap saying that was likely the most important lesson he could give about living in the swamp, or anywhere. Many a hunter, hard-shell swampers included, had died—or nearly so—from afearedness. Hamp did his best to wrestle the dread that clawed at him.

Duff prodded him with his foot. "Time to go, swamper."

When Hamp didn't budge, he shoved him harder.

More time! Hamp thought desperately. The more time he could steal, the better, to think everything through, to make a plan. Slowly he grabbled to his feet, hitching upright like a stiff-jointed old man. Halfway to standing he suddenly swooned, acted wobble-kneed and slumped down, moaning like a graveyard spook. "Guess I hain't got my legs back under me yet," he gasped.

Duff heaved a sigh, but let him be.

He lay on his side for a long while, rubbing the tenderness from the crusted lump on his scalp and staring up at the tops of the saplings that ringed the clearing. From there the branch tips of the hardwoods looked to be frothed with pale green foam, but were clusters of young leaves the size and shape of a newborn pup's ears. Bees hovered about a highbush huckleberry abloom with little white bells. They'd drop soon and scatter the ground like baby teeth, by midsummer replaced by fat blue-dusked berries Ma called rabbit eyes. They'd eat buckets of fresh, then she'd boil a kettleful with sugar to make jam. Everybody'd eat berries and jam till gum and tongue alike turned purple as Bone's.

His heart seized to think he mightn't be there for Ma's huckleberry jam. And he mightn't hear Pap play fiddle again, or play fox and geese with Neeta on the porch, or hear L.B. talk the first time. All the things he'd not do crowded in on him until he couldn't think of anything but them, nor do anything but pine after them.

Bone seemed to know and came to paw at him, whining and licking till he sat up. Satisfied Hamp wasn't sick or dead, he trotted off and hiked his leg at the base of a sapling and put a dark streak on its trunk. In a minute's time an orange butterfly flittered to the edge of the dark splot in the dirt and probed the dampness with its tongue.

Others drifted in and followed suit till it seemed a fine party, a butterfly frolic. Hamp had seen them ranked just the same way around puddles in the hog pen, but couldn't understand it.

Duff sat astraddle the log, pulling at a stick with his blade. Long curled shavings littered the ground at his feet so it looked like he'd gone and barbered a little blond girl of her ringlets. He'd been watching the butterflies, too. "That's purely vile. What kind of goodness might they be lapping up, do you think, swamper?"

Hamp shook his head as answer. The sight seemed to him a sign of sorts, but one past his power of reckoning.

As the sun climbed the sky toward late morning, his mind settled and scratched out a loose plan. He'd pretend to cozy up to Duff, be friendly and gain his trust. They'd move slow to the south, loop west through Grand Prairie and then turn northward, toward Rooter and Bugaboo, maybe even Billy's. He'd be sure and not let Duff figure out they were making a circle. With luck, somebody'd be out looking for him by Rooter or Bugaboo, or maybe they'd run into Scrub and Tate, though that seemed unlikely since they'd headed much farther west and planned to search the bigger thicks nearest Billy's.

Problem was, Duff wasn't scour-witted like them darkies Scrub always talked about, nor helpless like Tate said. He'd got pretty far into the swamp without help. Even so, no outlander—especially no darkie outlander— could outwit the swamp, or a swamper, forever. Many a thing could go wrong if you weren't careful: thickets and channels to get lost in, fanged vipers, gator holes, sucking mud. He'd lead Duff in harm's way and let the Okefenokee do what it wanted with him.

Duff grew fidgety and tired of the wait. He judged Hamp fit to travel and ordered him to his feet. There wasn't much in the way of trumpery to pack in the camp. Duff tucked his knife in the waist of his britches, then slung Pap's gun and shot bag and powder horn over his shoulder. Hamp carried the gunnysack, which held the flint box tucked in a leather pouch, and what was left of the duck, the bundle of colored feathers, the beat-up tin can and another little sack of things stowed behind the log.

When Duff turned his back, Hamp swiped a large hunk of charcoal from the fire and hid it in his britches pocket, glad of a sudden that their looseness hid the bulge of charcoal, and the bird whistle he'd taken, in creases and folds.

Duff shoved him ahead as they left the camp. "Lead on, but remember I got this gun on you. And I won't grieve if you make me put a slug in your gut."

And I'll not cry you when your time comes, Hamp told himself. I'll not care one lick.

They forged through scrub and thicket for a while till Hamp stumbled onto a narrow deer path carved through the brush. Split-hoof tracks pocked the dirt, so Hamp figured it was a main road for the island whitetails. Healed scars on some of the pine trunks showed sign of bucks that'd marked territory by rubbing the velvety skin from their new antlers during the fall rut.

The rough trail took them south and then curved slightly west. Hamp could feel it turn, though Duff didn't seem to notice. Yellow flies and biting gnats pestered them as the air warmed, and Hamp rolled down his sleeves to protect his arms. Duff pulled his hat low on his ears, but the bugs feasted on him through his ragged shirt, and he slapped himself ruddy. "They'll suck me dry as a strip of beef jerky before I make Florida," he muttered once, and to hear it put a bounce in Hamp's step.

Traveling put him at ease and gave his mind more time to work. Though every step trod now was new ground to him, it was ground he recognized, and he knew he could find his way in reverse if need came. His memory, and the charcoal marks, would guide him.

Pap had taught him to memorize land markers on the islands: an extra-big cypress topped by a hen hawk nest on one, three cypress close together toward the south end of another, a lightning-struck tree on the next. He set pictures of such markers fixed in his mind like beads strung of a certain order on a thread.

The deer trail finally opened at its south end into a cypress stand. Frilled with soft, new spring needles, the close-ranked cypresses cast shade on the wide, shallow bay of inky water beneath them. The still water reflected the high branches and patches of sky with mirrored exactness, punctured there and again by raised knobs of cypress knees fuzzy with green moss.

Behind Hamp the sound of Duff's footsteps fell to silence, and he peered back over his shoulder, hopeful the boy had taken a wrong turn and disappeared. But he was only a few steps back, hunkered down on his heels where the deer trail finished. He plucked something from the dirt and tipped his head back to study the treetops. In that moment Hamp slipped the charcoal from his pocket and struck a black crosshatch low across the trunk of a cypress tree to blaze it, for he knew the slight opening to the deer path would be close to invisible coming at it from the bay side.

"What did you find?" he called out, trying his best to sound friendly.

Duff pushed to his feet and called back, "Can you tell me what bird lost this, swamper?" He trotted to Hamp's side and opened his fingers to show a feather of the color found in blue iris petals or a deep summer sky.

Ma should have a ribbon of that color, Hamp thought. He'd buy it for her if fate turned and he brought Duff in to Tate. He took the feather and held it in the light so that it glistered jewel-like. "Indigo bird, we call it, but I heard it named bunting, too. Only the little cocks has this fancy color about them; the hens is drab brown."

Duff nodded. "Mama worked indigo fields on another plantation before Massa Tate bought her. Last time she saw any of her family was there . . ." His voice trailed away. Quickly he tucked the bird feather in the band of his hat and motioned for Hamp to move on.

They stopped past middle day to eat. Hamp's empty belly had begun to ache, and the ache traveled up and set a throb behind his eyes. They settled down on a patch of spongy ground at the foot of a cypress so wide and deeply ridged at the base, someone might've poured it onto the ground from up high, let it harden, then poured again to build it in the fashion of a wax candle that drips and puddles in its holder.

This time when Duff offered, Hamp took his portion of the roast duck and gnawed the bones clean. Bone sat on his haunches and watched, hopeful he'd get something thrown his way, but Hamp cracked the bones and sucked at the marrow, and licked the oil from his fingers. Bone's ears fell in disappointment, so Hamp held his hands out and let him slurp away the last traces.

Duff nibbled at his last piece. Though shreds of meat still clung to the bone, he tossed it toward Bone, who snatched it up and trotted a few feet away to finish it. He licked the oil from his own fingers.

Hamp lowered his face to the water and drank of it, savoring the faint bitter spike to it, how it cooled his throat. He splashed it over the back of his neck and on his cheeks, and dried himself with his sleeve.

Duff kneeled and cupped some water in his hands and sipped like he was drinking from a bowl. "Tastes like tea without sugar," he said. "Mistus liked it hot in the mornings, served up in a china cup thin as white paper, and biscuits with strawberry jam to go with it." He held his palm flat and lifted a pretend biscuit from it. He nibbled daintily and so ladylike that Hamp smiled before he could stop himself. Next Duff pinched the handle of a pretend cup and sipped properly, with raised pinky, but spewed when the imagined tea turned out to be too hot. Hamp let go a full laugh at the spectacle.

Duff cackled at his own joke, then rummaged in the gunnysack until he found the bundle of feathers and added the blue one to it. Dug farther and frowned. "Something's missing."

"What?" Hamp asked, leaning back on his elbows.

"A whistle. I must've dropped it."

Hamp worked to keep his features arranged straight. He got a sickish flutter deep in his belly. "Well, a whistle hain't so important a thing to lose, is it?"

"No," Duff answered, sullen. He banged his palm against his thigh. "It burns me all the same. I carved it special. Sumi loves any bird, and music, and I wanted to give it to her once I find her."

Hamp cocked his head back and stared up through the veil of green above them, hoping his voice sounded lighter than he felt. "My sister likes critters, too, but she likes ever one she meets—furred, feathered, scaly—it makes her no difference. . . . My pap's musical. Plays fiddle."

"Never met mine," Duff said. "Old Massa bought Mama when she was heavy with me. He took Sumi because she cried after Mama, but he didn't want Daddy. Left him at that indigo farm." He dropped the feathers in the gunnysack and tossed it at Hamp. "On your feet, swamper."

They traveled along the outskirts of the island, which was larger than Hamp imagined, maybe big as Billy's

Island. So long as they stayed to its hemline, he felt anchored, but beyond it Grand Prairie stretched wide and unknown as the sea. Once there he'd have to figure his way to loop around it. And so he wove them through the cypress bays in a wavy line such that a snake would take pride in, always choosing the worst route, the one to slow their pace.

But more than anything he did, it was the birds that caused Duff to hold up travel. He'd dally just to listen at birdsong, or watch them at their doings, or fetch another feather to his hatband. He called Hamp over to name them for him: blue scoggin, pipebill, flinthead, ramshack, tick-bird. Hamp savored the long minutes that passed while Duff studied and pondered, and he began to point out birds and songs Duff missed, just to feel the time slip away.

Toward day's end they came upon a tree full of squawking egrets. Egrets were common wading birds, white as cotton fluff with longish, stabbing beaks and bandy black legs, but even Hamp was captured by the sight of a hundred of them gathered on a single tree. Each seemed to own space enough to open its wings full out, wings Neeta said looked to be borrowed from angels. The tree branches trembled with their preening and their fussing and flapping, and the dark trunk was painted white and gray with their spatters.

"Roosting tree," Hamp whispered to Duff. "They knot up together like chickens do at night." Without thinking, he thrust out his neck and burst out a string of throaty squawks in mimic of the birds. He did it a second time. One of the birds tipped its head from side to side, drawing a bead with each ear on the sound, then dove headlong in their direction. Duff's eyes grew wider as it swooped within arm's reach and landed overhead. It gandered at them for a second before it flapped back to its roost in disappointment. A long, lacy feather drifted to the ground, and Duff caught it midair.

He looked at Hamp with a different expression to his face. "Can you do that for other birds?"

Hamp nodded. "Pap taught me hunting calls for duck and turkey gobblers, but I learned some others by listening."

Duff stroked the length of the white plume. "When I was little, Sumi told me that birds listen and carry our prayers to heaven when they fly. I asked her one day, 'How come it's so many prayers that ain't never answered?' She told me birds speak in a tongue we forgot long ago—way back when God cast the first folks out of His paradise. 'Birds, they remember, but we don't,' she said, 'so they can't always catch our words just right.'"

He carefully tucked the egret plume into his hatband. "Teach me to speak bird before we part ways, swamper. I want them to hear me, for once, and listen—for Sumi."

The flutter in Hamp's belly returned. He nodded agreement, but didn't trust himself to speak. How would their parting go? With both alive and one a prisoner, or with one of them dead?

At the very top of the egret tree, the largest of the

birds stopped preening and dipped its head. Its round, golden eye appeared to hold them both in its gaze, unblinking and stern.

Chapter 13

Shadows gathered, and the first wisps of mist scrolled from the water and reached out. Hamp and Duff struck camp on a patch of damp, spongy ground beneath a large cypress. There wasn't much to set up, no wood to make a fire. Duff took the chunk of smoked bacon Ma'd given him and shaved off two slivers. He handed one to Hamp, and they both tore into the strips, yanking and chewing the raw, salty meat.

Duff bit off half his and offered it to Bone on his palm. Darting eyes at Hamp, Bone craned his neck and took it in his grabber teeth with great politeness. Quick as a blink he tossed it back and swallowed without chewing.

"Stupid to feed good bacon to a dog," Hamp said. "Especially when there hain't hardly enough for the both of us."

Duff shrugged. "I know how it is to be hungry. Watch other folks eatin' fine when you ain't about to get nothing lest you can steal or scrounge it."

"Your master didn't feed you?"

"By his thinking, I guess he did," Duff answered, and then snorted. "Every Saturday Mistus would measure out cornmeal, sugar, salt and lard for each of the colored families. Never seemed to last long enough, no matter how we stretched it. Summers we put up a little garden back of our cabin with greens and yams and peas and okra. And I went along hunting with Massa's boys. They'd always give me something to take home: rabbits, turkeys, squirrels, coons. They didn't care about the wild meat, seeing as how they had plenty of ham and chickens and beeves to eat. When Mama helped cook for the big house, Mistus let us take the table scraps, even if Massa get after her about spoiling us. Any little extra we'd get, he counted against us."

Bone licked the oily salt off Duff's dangling fingers and sank to his haunches beside him. Duff stroked Bone's knobby head and silky ears. "You a good dog, ain't you, ol' boy?" he asked. "War's over, I be getting me a dog like you and spoiling him all I please. Ain't never had nothing, but first thing, I'll have me a dog."

Bone raked his tongue over Duff's hand and slapped his tail against the tree.

Hamp sucked his own fingers clean and scrubbed them across his britches. "Come, boy," he called. Bone obeyed, but cut his eyes at Duff before he did, in a manner that looked to Hamp like regret.

"Your pap fight in the war?" Duff asked. He picked up a stick and pulled the knife from his waist.

"From the start of it," Hamp answered, surprised at the note of pride that pushed its way into his voice. "Lost his leg up in Tennessee."

Duff grunted and shook his head. Wood shavings dropped between his knees. "War's over there'll be nothing but a country full of graves, peg legs, widows and orphans. And all us colored."

"You hope them Yanks win, don't you?" Hamp asked.

Duff shrugged and swiped his nose with the back of his hand, taking a measure of time before he answered. "Can't say as I trust any buchra, blue or gray. I trusted one, but he died. There'll not be another like him."

Hamp's eyes narrowed. "And what was the name of that one you trusted, Gavin?" It was the first time he'd used Duff's false name, and it seemed to ride the air like something solid and sharp: a fletched arrow.

Duff didn't give answer, but his brow and mouth took on angry furrows. He concentrated on drilling out the stick, on shaping out a mouthpiece to one end of it. Wood chips flew.

Somewhere in the dark a loon called to its mate with the sad, warbling tone made by a wooden Indian flute. Hamp cupped his hands so the fingers of each lay across the back of the other and his thumbs bent to cover the hollow between his palms. Touching thumbnails together, he rested his upper lip on the knuckles and gently blew down across the hollow, adjusted his hands until finally the sound of the loon warbled from them.

Kim L. Siegelson

In a moment the loon answered, its sad tune more hopeful now. Urgent.

Duff tapped the rough carved whistle against his leg to clear it, then blew through the mouthpiece. Bits of wood puffed from the holes at the top and end, followed by a low, hollow-toned hoot. A call less like the loon's and more that of the big-eared owl said to gather up the souls of them that died at night. Bone's ears pricked, and he lifted his chin and howled, wolfish and mournful.

Over and over they each sounded one and again till Hamp grew dizzy from blowing and fell back to watch the stars wheel overhead like a million silver water-skimmers circling on a dark and endless lake. The slivered moon cast only a little dry, brittle light, and there was not fire nor fatwood torch to push back the night.

Duff hooted once more, then rolled the new whistle between his fingers while he stared out at the darkness or the stars, Hamp wasn't sure which. He laid it aside and untied the loop of hemp twine that held up his britches. He squatted beside Hamp and pushed him to sitting. "Hands behind you," he said gruffly.

"You hain't gonna bind me, are you?" Hamp sputtered. It stung him to think Duff didn't trust him yet. And after he'd tried so hard all day to make him.

"Ain't personal, swamper. Like I said, there ain't a buchra alive who I trust, including you. Even with your bird talk."

The rough twine bit into Hamp's skin, and he couldn't

sleep with his arms drawn back like the pull-it bone of a chicken. And the little bird on the whistle barrel dug into the meat of his hip worse than the tree roots and twigs beneath him. Still, he closed his eyes and pretended sleep. Made his breathing deep and even, and smacked his lips like he was dreaming of something good to eat—Ma's rabbit stew, fried fish, corn pone, a baked yam. Fooled Bone, who snuck away to curl beside Duff.

He worked at the bindings on his wrists for a while, but did no more than rub his skin raw, and so stopped. Every now and again he opened his lids a slit to spy on Duff. He blended into the shadows well, though what moonlight there was glimmered on the curve of his cheek and forehead, or lit his eyes. He stayed up most of the night, whistling softly to himself, smoothing the barrel of the new carved whistle with pinches of grit, reaching out sometimes to pet Bone. But toward earliest mornglowm his head finally flopped to his shoulder and he slept.

Night was cold yet so early in the year, and it seeped into Hamp's bones through the damp bed of leaf litter he'd kicked up to rest in. He dozed off and on, but an achy numbness had settled in his arms and hands and kept him half wakeful till he gave up trying to sleep. He watched a line of dark clouds move in from the outlands, turning the dawn sky the color of damp metal. The air took on a sharp and rusty flavor. A wind ruffled the tree-tops, swaying the roosting white curlews and gray scoots who shuffled sidelong to the thicker end of their branches' nearest trunk and tucked heads beneath wings. Lightning pulsed behind the clouds, turning them a sallow yellow, like an old bruise. Thunder rumbled.

Duff cried out suddenly and bolted upright. "God above, help us, Gavin! Get down! Cannon fire!" He stared out at the darkness with wide, glazed eyes, panting like he'd run a distance.

Hamp's heart leapt, not from fear but surprise. It did the same when Pap woke up at night like that, yelling people's names, talking gibberish, cursing. Ma calmed him, talked soft and coaxed him back to bed. He'd listened to her in the dark, had heard Pap weeping in her arms, even wailing. It turned his stomach to remember. Hearing Pap do such things afeared him worse than any other thing he could think of.

Now it scared him to see Duff, shivering and shaking with tremors. His face looked pale as wood ash, with an anguished gash for a mouth, and teeth a-chatter.

Hamp remembered the soft way Ma handled Pap and spoke to him. With hands bound he could only speak. "Easy, it hain't but thunder," he said. "Only God's thunder, not man's." He said it over and over until Duff's shivering slowed and he pulled in long ragged breaths.

Duff fumbled for the musket lying beside him and held it close to his leg. "Sounded like cannon. Can't get the echo of it out from my head. I keep thinking if I go farther away, maybe it'll quiet. But damned if it don't track me and tear into me like a dog on a rabbit."

He covered his face with his open hand and lay back, rocked from side to side for a while, then curled and pushed his face to Bone's ribs. "Good old dog," he murmured. "Good old boy."

"It's coming a freshet," Hamp said at the next clap of thunder, though he knew the storms of late always passed by. "We best move inland and build shelter to wait it out."

Duff was right—there couldn't ever be any real trust between them. He'd let himself get too friendly. For a little while he'd even allowed the idea that the journey was an adventure. But the twine cutting into his wrists pointed to something different. It reminded him that Duff was a kidnapper, as well as a murderer.

Before another boom rattled off, Duff gathered his wits and loosed Hamp's wrist bindings. They snatched up trumpery and tackle and set off in a northwesterly direction, away from the swampy woods in favor of the dry hummocks and piney woods. They'd not gone far when they passed through a narrow strip of sand scrub smattered with loblolly and pond pine and palmetto, and reached a young hummock of water oak and sweet gum and bay saplings. It'd not taken near the time Hamp hoped, for it wasn't yet fully morn, but tottering still at the brink of one day and the next, where moon and sun faced like duelers.

A dampening rain misted the air without falling to ground and brought with it the scent of old brown coppers held long in a closed fist. Duff's hat had turned dark in patches and his arms shone slick as oil. "I'll watch you build," he told Hamp, hefting the musket to the crook of his arm.

Hamp shed the haversack onto the leaf litter and scoured the edges of the hummock for limbs. He found three of length taller than him and lashed them with vines of possum grape to two saplings so they formed the frame of a small lean-to. He snapped myrtle branches and laid those crossways on the frame, weaving and bending them into a mesh over the frame.

"I need to thatch it with palmetto fans," he said. "They'll shed the water, but it'll take a blade to hack through the stems."

Duff hesitated, then drew the knife from his waist and tossed it in the dirt at Hamp's feet. He leveled the gun at him and Hamp saw that he'd covered the pan with a large leaf to keep the powder dry. "I'll follow you, swamper."

Hamp worked slow, muttering curses at Duff. The knife blade was dulled from whittling and the fibrous stems of the palmetto were tough to hack through. But the little teeth along the margins of the leaf stems cut his palms easy as butter. He stopped often to wipe blood on his britches, or rain and sweat from his eyes with the back of his wrist. His nerves grew tight-strung with the feel of a gun barrel on him, and from fighting the instinct to bolt like a rabbit.

Wind gusts riffled the palmettos into gray-green waves around him that clattered and hissed. When he finally judged the pile of cut fans enough, he gathered them by their long stems and dragged them behind like a sled.

Suddenly Duff raised the gun to his shoulder and yelled, "Stop! Don't step again!"

Bewildered, Hamp let go the stems and raised his hands, stumbled a half step forward. In that moment the single dark and steady eye of the rifle flashed. A loud crack followed and echoed through the trees. Duff jerked backward as Hamp's breath left him in a sudden, high-pitched wail. A spray of dirt flung up in his face as he fell to his right side and bright pain shot through his hip.

Chapter 14

Blinded by grit, Hamp waited to feel a rush of warm blood or new pain, but felt nothing past the stabbing in his hip. He heard Bone barking up a calaberment, and the cry of startled birds, and the rustle of Duff moving through the palmetto toward him. He lay quiet, playing dead like a possum, even when Duff bent and took the closed blade from his limp hand and stepped back. Maybe he'd go away, leave his body for the buzzards to pick at.

"You swooned?" he asked, shoving Hamp with his toe. When Hamp neither moved nor answered, Duff heaved a sigh. "You ain't shot, swamper."

Bone noozled Hamp and pawed at him and tongue-scoured his ear and neck till Hamp shoved him off and sat up. He probed his hip and realized he'd but fallen atop the whistle. His eyes stung and his chest felt aflame with pure anger, his throat choked by it. "If I hain't shot, it's only 'cause you can't aim worth a Yankee cent!"

Duff snorted and poked his jaw out. "Tell that to the snake you was about to trod over. I'll wager he don't agree with you a'tall."

It lay a few steps from where Hamp had fallen, still as a pine limb, thick as a man's arm and longer than either him or Duff were tall. The raw, headless neck stub at one end glistered with a sugary coating of pale sand, and the row of rattle buttons at its tail end was the length of a middle finger. It'd not used them to warn him off, though.

"Biggest diamondback rattler I ever seen," Hamp said, awed and shaken. Had it emptied its fangs in him, he'd be no more than food for beetles and jackdaws by nightfall. Some words of thanks formed in his mind, but he couldn't wrap his mouth around them. Duff had saved him, true, but for a selfish reason—he needed a guide. Did the one thing balance the other? He took the viper by the tail buttons, slung it atop the bundle of palmetto fans and dragged it along to the lean-to, his thoughts muddled.

It took no time to layer the fans over the myrtle boughs, and there was overhang enough to kindle a smoky fire of damp twigs and pinecones. Duff greased the musket with the rind from the bacon and reloaded it with fresh powder and slug while Hamp gutted and skinned the snake outside. He pinned its hide to a sapling trunk with water locust thorns and reflected again on its death in trade for his, by Duff's hand. Did it beholden him now to a murderer?

He speared chunks of the white snake flesh onto sharp green-wood sticks and held them over the fire, scarcely able to wait for them to roast and curl at the edges before tearing into them. He and Duff and Bone ate of it until their stomachs stretched round and taut as ripe summer melons, and still there was meat to be cooked and stowed in the sack that'd held the duck carcass.

They lay back with arms crossed behind their heads and closed their eyes. Hamp wondered if Duff would bind him or keep watch, but when he peeked from his eye corner, Duff looked peaceful, unconcerned. He'd pulled his hat over his face and was humming softly. Bone had curled between them so he touched them both, but rested his head on Duff's thighs.

Hamp slid his hand to his waist. Duff had given him the blade to skin the snake and he'd not given it back yet. He fingered the smooth haft down to where the warm wood and cold metal joined. Duff turned the full span of his back toward Hamp and drew his knees up so the bend of his legs cradled the curve of Bone's body.

Water pattered and matched rhythm with Hamp's heart as he drew the knife out. He rolled to face Duff's back and pondered its landscape: dark skin divided by the knobbed ridge of spine, the dips between ribs that shallowed and deepened with the rise and fall of breathing, blunt shoulder blades, forest of woolly hair that began at the neck's nape and disappeared beneath the hat. Hamp

Kim L. Siegelson

watched the small muscles of Duff's back ripple as he shifted himself to a more comfortable arrangement. He closed his eyes, for the snake meat felt as if it'd come back to squirming life in his belly.

One hard jab would do it—left side beneath the shoulder blade, sweet spot on a deer. He fisted the knife handle and opened his eyes to stare at the spot, at the smooth skin and fine hairs that looked nothing like a deer's, only like a boy's. The metal blade of the knife was etched with rust and snake gore, but the name engraved in curled letters was clear: GAVIN TATE. What final justice to push Gavin's blade into the one who'd murdered him, to let it bring what pain and suffering he deserved, let snake blood mingle with his.

But he couldn't. Even if this was his only chance. He couldn't bring himself to thank Duff aloud for sparing him the viper's sting, and so this quiet, secret way would have to serve. Only him and God would know, and maybe Gavin, if spirits had such powers once they'd left earth.

He rolled away and tucked the knife at his waist, but held his hand pressed to its haft, wondering on the soldier boy who'd carried it once. Was Gavin looking down and wishing to be avenged? Did the dead care, or was it only the living ones who did? His mind churned with questions that hadn't clear answers, and some that might. But only Duff could answer those.

"You was yelling for Gavin in your dreams this morning," he said, hesitantly breaking the silence. "That hain't your name, is it?"

Duff hauled himself to sitting with both knees pulled up against his chest and his arms round them. He appeared to wrestle with himself over what answer to give, then finally said, "You remember asking me to name for you who it was I trusted? That's his name—Gavin."

"Then what's yours?" To Hamp's mind, Duff's answer seemed greatly important. He wanted to hear him tell one small truth, even if it was only his name. Somehow it might be the pintle to help join them, a pivot point of trust.

Duff stared at him hard, then looked away. He held his hand palm up outside the lean-to and squinted up at the sky. "Storm didn't amount to more than a drizzle, and now half the day's gone to waste." Before he crawled outside, he tugged his hat down over his ears and rubbed Bone's tight belly.

• • •

They backtracked at a hurried pace until they reached the southwest edge of the island near where they'd gone inland. Beyond it stretched Grand Prairie. All islands that dotted it and channels that coursed through it were unnamed to Hamp, and he stood for a moment before the vista in quiet panic. So far he'd not allowed himself to feel so, but he could not quell the sudden flood of fear that rose up. To go forward meant stepping off the rim of what was familiar and known. He wished it was Pap traveling beside him, acting as guide. For it to be adventure instead of what it was.

But there was nothing to do now but go forward, stay

Kim L. Siegelson

with his plan to kill time, slowly circle west and hope for the best. He set sight on a small, treeless tussock of maiden cane and pickerelweed, drew up a deep breath and slogged at it through a raft of yellow-blossomed hardheads and drifts of bladderwort. When they gained that tussock, they set out for another, and another again in the pattern of checker pawns moved over a board. Staying to the shallows and solid ground as much as possible, he made one move south, two west in what he hoped was a sly diagonal. He marked the distance in passing of time: third of a day from the island where Duff captured him, half a day from Rooter, a whole day from Bugaboo. Not too far away from Pinder yet.

Then came another night, and another day, and another till Hamp could no longer fool himself into imagining that Pinder was close. The cord that bound him to it felt stretched and frayed.

At evenfall on the third day, they reached a treed prairie head of size large enough to name, and there stopped in a clearing of pines. Neither he nor Duff had chatted much during the hard traveling, and they spoke little while gathering limbs to kindle a fire on a bald patch of sandy ground.

Beneath the trees to the back of the clearing the ground rose up in a mound shaped like a turtle shell and big around as three punts laid end to end. Trees thick as house poles grew from its center as a sign of its age. The folks on Billy's Island had cut into a similar mound with a spade and found Indian relics buried inside. What purpose the mounds once had baffled them all. Was it holy site, burial ground or ancient trash heap? No one he knew could say for certain.

Pap said the mound builders had been gone from the swamp a long time. But Hamp wondered if there might be an old one somewhere who remembered this place and spoke its name from memory, yearning for what was lost. It unsettled him to think how quickly the swamp claimed itself and forgot even them that'd named it first. He circled the bounds of the mound, collecting dropped wood, but did not set foot to climb atop.

When the fire was kindled, he added green myrtle leaves to the flames and hunkered close to the billows of smoke as remedy against mosquitoes. Wisps of steam rose from his clothes and Duff's so that they each looked to be a-smolder with some hidden and personal fire.

They ate cold nuggets of roast snake from their palms and tossed some to Bone. Then Duff picked up a stick and reached to his waist for his knife. He looked up quick, his eyes hard as two black pebbles set in his face. "You stole my knife!"

"I didn't!" Hamp shot back, stung by the charge. He drew out the knife, but didn't offer it. "You didn't never ask it back from me."

"Give me my knife," Duff said, his voice low and hot. The fire cast flickering shadows and orange light upward on his face so that he looked demonish and chiseled by hate. He fumbled a hand back toward the musket.

Hamp balanced the blade in his hand, measuring its

Kim L. Siegelson

weight. It was no match for the musket should Duff level its blank eye at him again. He tossed the knife across the fire into the sand so that its point stuck in the dirt near the extra toe on Duff's left foot.

Duff snatched it up and spit-polished it with the tatty hem of his shirt, then held it close to the dying fire to inspect it. As he turned it over in his hands, it flashed fire-light in his face. He sagged in his skin like an old widower, and shoved the stick he'd planned on whittling into the fire so that it flared and sent up a shower of sparks. "Just, I ain't want to lose this."

Hamp grunted and spat in the fire as statement enough. He'd not give sympathy Duff didn't deserve. "You probably stole that blade," he said, taunting. "Like you stole the name etched on it, too."

Duff canted his head back a notch, studying Hamp from under hooded lids. The sides of his nose flared, and his hands trembled with pent rage. "This knife was gifted to me by Gavin. I ain't stole nothing!"

Hamp heaved a sigh like he did when Scrub started in on a rambling story he didn't care to hear. "How am I to believe it when you hain't told but lies since I met you?"

Duff laid the knife on the flat of his palm and closed his fingers around it so hard, Hamp winced. His voice rasped when he spoke. "Old Massa Tate gifted me to his youngest boy, the name set on this blade, and wasn't no different from giving him a horse or hunting dog. 'Daddy, give him to me,' Gavin begged. I was thirteen and him twelve that year. So Massa give him my papers, easy as that." He opened his hand again so the knife lay cradled in it. Two straight red lines marked his skin where he'd gripped the blade.

"It didn't bother me then. I liked Gavin. Him and me come up together on the farm, side by side. He give me this knife when he joined the Rebs. That's the plain truth of it."

"Why so?" Hamp wondered. "He needed it worse than you, I'll wager."

Duff shrugged. "He had a gun. Rebs wouldn't let me carry one—no coloreds is allowed to be carrying guns. Gavin joked how I was the truer aim, but he got the gun and uniform. Was a joke neither of us laughed at for long. Still, I needed something if I was to be with him so close to battles, so he handed me this."

"He give up his own knife so you could protect yourself," Hamp said, probing. "You must've been good friends, huh?" He wanted to shame Duff, and he wanted Duff to be sorry. If only he'd show a scrap of guilt over what treachery he'd done.

Duff shook his head and looked off. "Friends mightn't be the right word. Not friends where him and me is equals, and both of us is got a choice about it." He let the knife dangle loose in his fingers. "When we was little boys and my mama watched after us together, I thought so. Back then we didn't know a thing except run the fields, fish at the creek, jump in the cotton bin, laugh at the same things and answer Mama when she called. And it felt like friends when Massa Gavin taught me to shoot in secret and didn't mind I was better at it. And when he taught me to read and write a little bit behind his daddy's back. He risked a whipping with a razor strop for it, so I tried never to make trouble for him. But it's always in my head that he is boss, and I ain't free to go. Ain't free to speak my mind. Is that how it is with friends?"

"But he was the one you said you trusted," Hamp offered.

Duff's face chiseled hard again, and his mouth twisted like he'd chewed on something bitter. "War changed that. Made him different. I shouldn't have gone with him."

"Why did you?"

"Foolishness. To be somewhere other than the farm. Gavin asked me, and Mistus, too. Said it'd be a thing to talk about when we was old men, how we was a part of the big war for Southern independence. He figured on me still being with him when we was old. . . .

"And I started thinking that over. About how he could keep me long as he wanted. Till we's both of us gray-beards, and I got no say in it. Ain't the Yankees promising me my independence? It sure ain't Gavin nor a one of the Rebs. All they's wanting is to keep me down with their foot on my neck!"

"Nosir!" Hamp broke in, his voice rising. "My pap didn't fight to keep you down. He hain't never owned a slave, don't truck with it, and it'd burn him to hear you say he did. You said yourself the Yankees don't treat

Negras no better. They hain't fighting for you. The whole of it is they want to force the South to stay bound with the North. The Yankees invaded us and give us no choice but fight back. All we want is freedom."

Duff leaned in until his nose nearly touched Hamp's. "I want the same thing, swamper. What reason the Yanks got to march down here don't matter to me, and what reason your pap had to fight 'em don't, neither. Fact is, if gray wins this war, I lose, and if blue wins, I win. Me and Sumi and Mama will be free by law."

Hamp recalled Angus Tate's telling of the beating laid on Duff's ma for Gavin's death, and his promise to find Duff and make him suffer, and make every runaway suffer as a traitor, too. If the Yankees won, there'd be many more like the Tates who'd take their revenge on Negras. Surely Duff knew so. "Freedom mightn't be worth the price you pay for it."

Duff smiled, the patient sort reserved for babies and fools. "According to you, all them Rebel farmers out fighting Yanks thinks freedom to be worth a high price. It ain't worth no less to me, and maybe more. I'd as soon die right here than go back to slaving for the Tates."

They both fell quiet. Sat still, listening to the squealed complaints of the wood as it burned in the liquid, dancing flames of the fire between them.

"I wish the war was done with, one way or the other," Hamp said finally. His voice sounded flat and far-off in his ears.

"I wish it, too," Duff agreed, gazing through slotted eyes at the fire.

"You hain't told me your real name yet."

Duff raked his teeth over his lower lip. "Take your pick," he answered. " 'Tate's boy' is what most buchra call me. And 'Duff' is what name Tate give me when I was born. It's the name Gavin called me by. But I found out *duff* is a word for the leaf trash on the ground." He paused. "I decided I'll choose one to suit me better, now I'm free."

Hamp wondered what name in all the world he'd pick for himself if he could change it. It'd be hard to decide. "What name did you choose?" he asked Duff.

Duff pinchered his lips in gesture of buttoning them. "Secret," he answered. "Mama said to take care the first time you speak a newborn's name, for all who hear it are soul-linked to it forever. I be starting over and making a new life in Florida. I want Sumi to be the first to hear my chosen name. I ain't trusting none but her when I say it."

With that he rose and cinched Hamp's hands behind him with the twine, palms pressed together in flipped arrangement of prayer. Too tight to wiggle free, but loose enough this time for blood to flow beneath the bindings.

The fire burned away to glowing embers. Darkness pressed in so close that it seemed to Hamp they'd been swallowed up and were lodged inside the craw of a creature bigger than Jonah's whale. He'd soon be dissolved by it. He wanted to be spit out on some firm shore where he could find his way home to Pinder. Duff could disappear into the swamp like a will-o-the-wisp. Angus Tate could keep his gold coins. What they'd buy amounted to scrimptious little, and nothing important. They'd not fix Pap, nor turn the war, nor bring back Gavin Tate.

It shamed him to think he'd ever prayed for Neeta to be taken away. For Pap to be dead. He pressed his eyes shut and thanked God for ignoring him, for knowing not to answer the prayers of fools. He didn't want to take another step away from home.

Surely by now Ma and Pap were worried something wasn't right. He hoped Neeta would tell and there'd be a search for him. His heart told him that she would, and that someone would come for him.

But sudden hope mingled with dread.

Neeta would have to tell that he'd taken Scrub's runaways to Bugaboo and there they'd find Ruth and Julius and Mercy. Unless they'd gone . . .

But he'd heard Julius say they'd stay awhile and rest before they headed out—maybe several days. Four days had passed since then, though it felt like more. He prayed with all his soul that Angus Tate and his league were still on the wrong path, and looking for Duff. Not called back to search for him. And he prayed most of all that God hadn't given up listening to him just yet.

Chapter 15

When Hamp woke, the first wash of gray light tinted the sky. His last thought before sleep had been of Julius and Ruth and little Mercy out on Bugaboo Island, and so was his first. Were they asleep, thinking they were safe like he'd told them they'd be? He wished for a way to warn them into hiding or running so they'd not be found if someone came looking for him. He dreaded traveling anew, adding more distance.

Even if he could escape Duff, it'd take almost a day to backtrack by foot to Bugaboo, though this time he'd travel a straight, fast line. By then it might be too late to help the runaways, but he craved a chance to try. Couldn't get it out of his thinking.

Duff had got up early, or maybe hadn't slept, for a newly stoked fire crackled atop the ash heap as ward against the morning's damp chill. He tossed a kindling stick toward the clearing edge for Bone to scramble after and bring back in a game of fetch, like they hadn't any burdens at all. Each time Bone dropped the stick at his feet, Duff scratched his ears or stroked his back, and once bent to peck his topknot in a way that reminded Hamp of Ma kissing L.B. He stopped once to listen to a black-headed tick-bird scold Bone. He tried to mimic its voice, *phee-bee, phee-bee,* but it came out too nasal and squeaky, and the bird flittered into the brush like it'd been insulted. Bone canted his head side to side in a look of pure puzzlement that made Duff burst out laughing.

He seemed more at ease, whereas Hamp felt weighted with extra burdens. His shoulders ached, and his hands were stiff with cold from sleeping curled like a hound with his face to the coals all night, wrists bound behind him. He struggled to sit and then turned so his fingertips might take some heat and start to thaw.

Duff quieted and flung the stick toward the Indian mound. Bone fetched it but trotted past him and dropped it before Hamp, waggled his rump end and cut his eyes from stick to Hamp's face. He took it as a token of loyalty, and had his arms not been tied, he'd have hugged them around Bone's neck, but he could do nothing until Duff let him a-loose. Nothing but glower, and cuss him in silence.

"Don't you give me that evil eye, young man," Duff said, using the voice of a stern old woman.

"My hands is frozen and I got to pee," Hamp gave as reason, which wasn't false.

Bone swiveled his head again at Duff and groaned, then shook his ears so they clapped together. Duff pretend-scowled and shook his finger at him. "No lip from you, either, boy! Straighten up or I'll make a field hand out of you!"

Hamp scooted backward when Duff came near. Worried that he'd gone off kilter and turned addle-headed.

Duff rolled his eyes. "Old Mistus sounds like that.

Kim L. Siegelson

Don't you swampers ever fool, or is every one as sour-natured as you?"

"Sorry," Hamp mumbled. The word stood alone for all his feelings. It seemed longer than days since he'd left Neeta standing in the glow of the torchlight on the path home in favor of following Duff. "Sorry," he said again.

With dampened mood Duff untied him and watched with the musket in hand while he took privacy in the thick. Some of the smaller saplings in the thick had died standing so that they looked like fleshless hands reaching up in a gesture of pleading. The ground beneath them was plowed and gullied up in troughs and pits that bared their roots naked. He wondered if such deep scrapes were made by an extra-big buck during rutting season as a way of marking territory. But the lack of antler rubs on the trunks argued against deer, so he reckoned bears searching for grubs had done the digging.

"Nothing left but cracked corn to eat," Duff said when Hamp joined him again by the fire.

Hamp felt cored out, but not from hunger. His thoughts ran toward Julius and Ruth. He couldn't shake them from his mind, nor could he rid himself of Angus Tate's voice railing against runaways. Scrub had led Tate's party wrong. He'd know that soon as he got to Billy's and talked with the swampers there, sure enough. Then they'd backtrack to Pinder, and Pap would point them toward Rooter. By then maybe they'd be worried about him, and Neeta would say what they'd done. They'd follow his tracks to Julius and Ruth on Bugaboo first.

He could see it in his mind clear as looking through glass: Tate's rage at losing Duff, him serving Duff's punishment on the three of them like his daddy had served it on Duff's ma. Nobody to stop him, or to signal Julius and Ruth of the storm coming.

He only half listened to Duff, nodded agreement that they'd boil a handful of the corn in the tin and take turns sipping the gruel, then not eat again. He couldn't speak for fear of blurting what he'd decided: he'd travel no farther with Duff. He had to turn back and get to Bugaboo before someone else did.

Thin, gauzy fog turned the woods soft at the edges so it seemed as if they walked together through a dreamland, hushed but for peepers and bullfrogs. It didn't take long to reach a strand of water that unraveled from a larger channel clotted with never-wets and lilies. Five ducks paddled an aimless circle at the center, three with heads tucked to their breasts so they appeared not to have one. While Duff scooped water into the tin, Hamp wandered aside with Bone, his heart clambering at the prospect of running. "I'll see can I find a duck's nest," he called out. "Boiled eggs would be good."

He pretended to scour the bank, poking into the maiden cane and clumped rushes, gathering nerve to break and run. From his eye corner he saw Duff stand with the full tin and watch after him. He turned and lifted his hand in hopes of setting him at ease. Duff smiled and lifted the tin the way men did at frolics when toasting each other with wine brewed from possum grapes.

Kim L. Siegelson

Hamp fixed his eyes on a bend in the channel where the rush and spike grasses bristled extra thick, and plunged toward it, wondering how much more distance Duff would trust him to take. As he parted the rushes, a fury of feathers exploded from the heart of it, wings beating his face. He yelped and fell back hard enough to knock breath from him. Bone reared up on his dewclaws, barking, and the ducks on the water skittered to the far edge of the strand.

"What happened?" Duff called, a note of worry in his voice.

Hamp answered quickly to stop Duff from coming closer. "Surprised a nesting duck!"

He stood and brushed himself off, and pushed aside the stalks to gaze on the treasure he'd seen hidden. Inside the tangle was an old Indian boat, a dugout carved from a long cypress log, big enough to hold three or four people with room for trumpery, too. The grainy wood was weathered to pale gray and pied with spots of green moss. But it hadn't yet begun to melt into the swamp and mightn't for another hundred years or more, such was the strength of cypress against rot. Two long-bladed paddles, one broken short at the handle, lay beneath the nest litter of many past generations of ducks. A new, down-lined nest of bent grass cupped three greenish eggs.

"Did you find something?" Duff called out, starting toward him.

Hamp plucked the warm eggs up and held them high so Duff could see. Before he stepped back from the dugout and let the rushes rank together around it as they'd been, he felt in his pocket for the ribbon of cloth torn from Duff's shirt, the one left in the shed on Pinder. He tied it to a stalk as marker.

It was barely mornglowm, with the slip of moon still visible in the sky, and the morning birds not yet in full song. He'd have time to slip away and come back to the dugout without Duff. Then they'd both be free to go their own ways. Julius and Ruth and Mercy should be, too.

How far was Bugaboo by boat? He wasn't certain, only knew that three days had passed since he'd left the hunting camp. Truth was, it didn't matter. Nothing did but taking that dugout and leaving Duff. With luck, he'd reach Bugaboo in time to save Julius and Ruth; if not, at least he'd save himself.

Back at the camp, Duff wetted his shirt with water, wiped the flecks of duck dung from the eggs and put them in the tin to boil. He puttered about, whistling a tune Hamp took to be of his own making, for it was punctuated in places with birdcalls of a type Hamp couldn't place other than they might be warbler.

When he judged the eggs boiled to doneness, he fished them out with a forked stick. He kept one and gave the other two to Hamp. "You ought to get the bigger share for finding them," he said, and then cackled. "I thought for sure I was going to have to save your hide again, waste a bullet on something. You turned whiter than any living buchra I ever seen when that duck flew up at you!"

Hamp couldn't help scowling. "You don't have to save

me. I can take care of myself in this swamp just fine. It's me that lives here."

"That's why I got to save you," Duff answered. "You're my guide . . . and sometimes you ain't bad company, besides. When you ain't acting sour, you remind me of Gavin."

Why did you kill him? Hamp formed the question in his mind, but didn't ask. Because it didn't matter anymore. Gavin was dead and gone, same as a lot of others who'd gone off to fight.

He rolled one of the eggs between his palms, savoring its warmth and its smoothness before he cracked it. He dropped the flakes of shell in a pile between his legs and, when it was clean, held it on his palm so Bone could take it.

A sudden thought came to him: he might have to go without Bone. There'd likely be no time to wait or search for him. And it'd alert Duff if Hamp called out or whistled for Bone.

With leaden heart he cracked the second egg and peeled it and held that one out for Bone, too. Duff's smile faded to puzzlement, but he said nothing. He ate his own egg in three bites and then dumped the water from the tin onto the coals of the fire so that a hissing plume of steam hurtled upward toward the clouds that were beginning to stack up thick as baled cotton.

The little breeze that picked up and blew toward them had a odd scent to it. Musky as a pigpen but mixed with the sharp fruitiness of apple cider and the stench of an outhouse. Bone lifted his head and growled. His ears pulled up toward the top of his head as he got to his feet and lifted his nose up high. He sniffed deeply, then whined and tucked his tail.

Duff reeled him back to sitting and put a hand over his muzzle to quiet him. "There's someone out there," he whispered. "Stay still and quiet."

But for the rustling leaves and the low sizzling of the wet fire, all was strangely quiet, like the island was holding its breath with them. The smell ripened, and sudden fear seized Hamp. Before he could speak, a group of bristle-backed hogs trotted into the far side of the clearing from the Indian mound and stopped at the edge.

All parts of Hamp stopped working at once: voice, heartbeat, mind, legs. Though flesh covered them, their skulls matched the one that hung over Scrub's mantel. "Rooters!" he whispered, even though he meant to yell warning.

They banded up in an anxious clot, grunting and squealing and working air through the blunt end of their snouts. Most were sows no bigger than regular hogs, but all had thick pelts of dark bristles, and eyes like pepper-corns set in each side of their skulls. Bone broke free of Duff and rushed at them, barking and snapping at the air. The harem of sows, along with their shoats and piglets, scrambled back into the tree thick. Hamp whistled for Bone to come away, relieved and proud he'd scattered the rooters so easily.

Bone retreated a few steps, but not many before a

broad-shouldered boar rooter trotted from the cover. It was heavy-bodied, the size of a yearling calf, and pelted with graying bristles. Its head seemed far too large for its tiny eyes, the skull nearly big as a watering trough. Two tusks jutted from its lower jaw like curved shards of gray flint. Most of one spade-shaped ear was missing, and the other was taggy with old wounds. The beast twisted them atop his head as he sized things up, taking measure of enemies by scent and sound more than by sight.

"Get up a tree!" Hamp hollered, looking for one near enough to climb. His heart sunk to see mostly saplings. If the bristle-back came for him, he'd have to run. Hadn't Pap told him once that zigzagging was the best way? He couldn't recall, but it sounded right.

Duff snatched the musket and shinned up a fair-sized pine until he reached a sturdy branch. In a flash, Hamp grabbed the shot bag Duff had left lying atop the gunny-sack and threw it over his neck. Before he could get to Bone, haul him up a tree if he had to, Bone darted forward. The boar snorted and wagged its head, drawing a bead with each eye. It studied Hamp first, and then Bone, seeming to weigh what danger each of them posed, trying to decide which to take on.

Bone stood on his hind legs, boxing the air and snarling at the boar. He barked and carried on till foam gathered at the corners of his mouth. Hamp watched, frozen, as the boar fixed on Bone. It grunted loud and charged, its hooves churning over the ground as it rushed forward.

Bone leapt away at the last second, but his feet tangled in the jumble of unburned wood piled near the fire. In blinks of slow time Hamp saw the pig lower its slab of a head and sling sideways as it raced by. The force of the passing blow sent Bone smashing into the trunk of a pond locust. He screamed and fell to the dirt. A deep gash in his right flank gushed bright blood.

Hamp found his voice and yelled up at Duff, "By God, shoot it!" He sounded strange to himself, high-pitched as Neeta. Desperate like Pap waking from a nightmare.

Duff raised the gun to his shoulder as the boar crashed to a stop in the brush and turned back. But he didn't fire, dropped his sight from the hog to look down at Hamp.

"What are you doing?" Hamp cried. "It'll kill him!"

Storm clouds gathered behind Duff's eyes. "One shot left. You took the slugs and powder. Says to me you'll run off soon as I pull the trigger. Am I right?"

Hamp didn't answer. He couldn't think.

The smell of dog blood had brought the smaller pigs in closer, and Hamp could see their lean, gray forms at the edge of the clearing. Waiting. Bone wobbled to his feet and stood on three legs. His back end slumped suddenly, but he caught himself and, tottering, tried to stand his ground again. For certain he'd be run into the dirt beneath the boar's hooves, but he bared his teeth as the beast turned toward him for a second run.

"Hamp!" Duff yelled, leveling the gun on him. "Don't make me choose!"

Hamp's breath tore through him as the hog raced for-

Kim L. Siegelson

ward. He blinked back the stinging heat rising behind his eyes. No matter what, he'd not be like Pap. He'd hold his tears, never let Duff nor nobody else ever see him cry. But he'd curse Duff all his days, even with his dying breath.

Chapter 16

A quick flash and an explosion cracked the air across from Hamp. Though his eyes were fixed on Bone, he saw Duff flip backward from the pine tree like a can knocked from a fence rail. At nearly the same moment the legs of the charging boar buckled under and it slid gruntle first into the locust tree beside Bone, knocking his feet from beneath him.

The rooters in the thick scattered, squealing and bawling as they clambered a path through the brush.

In ten steps Hamp reached Bone and slid his hand under his head. Beside him the boar still breathed. He felt the heat from its body. Duff's shot had hit it in the thick of its neck, shattering its spine and throat. It'd not live long.

Duff moaned and gasped for breath at the base of the pine. He lay in a sprawl atop the gun. He pulled it from beneath him, and the effort of it put a grimace across his face. "I cracked my side," he panted as he tried to sit up. "My leg's hurt, too."

Hamp pondered him, letting what rage was left inside loosen its grip. He could take Bone and go now. Let all this be over. He could paddle the old dugout to Bugaboo, then home to Pinder. Duff couldn't stop him anymore.

Duff scooted himself up against the base of the pine he'd fallen from. Sweat beaded along his hairline and ran rivulets beside his ears. Bone struggled to stand and then limped over to him. He licked the salt from Duff's cheek and pushed his muzzle into Duff's hand.

"You a good, brave dog," Duff choked, the words squeezing from between gritted teeth. "Brave to keep that hog from charging your master. Brave as any soldier I seen."

Bone collapsed beside him and gnawed at the gash on his flank, whimpering and trembling.

"Here, boy," Hamp called out, not wanting to get close to Duff. "We can go now."

Bone's wet, brown eyes searched Hamp's before he rested his chin on Duff's lap. For the first time ever, he didn't do as Hamp bade him. He'd always led Hamp right, had saved him more than one time in the swamp. But Bone didn't understand everything. He didn't know what Duff had done, that he was a murderer and a traitor.

He'd saved Bone when he didn't have to, though, even though he knew Hamp would go. And he'd shot the viper

Kim L. Siegelson

rather than let Hamp step on it. Hamp owed him for those things. He searched his mind for Pap's voice, the Pap he missed, the one who'd know the right thing. It came to him so clear and sudden, he felt his heart gallop a few paces. *Don't be afraid to change course when your gut says you ought to.*

He didn't know how else to understand, or to decide, and so said, "I know you killed Gavin Tate, and I want to know why."

Duff looked like he stopped breathing. "Who told you that?"

Hamp stared him down. "His brother, Lieutenant Angus Tate. He's on your tail and looking to take your head off, and any other runaway's he comes across."

Duff closed his eyes and set his jaw. "You won't believe me, no matter what I say." He grimaced with pain, and tossed the gun at Hamp. "Leave, or go ahead and kill me. I'd rather it be you than Tate anyway."

Hamp picked up the gun and ran his hand over the barrel. He couldn't bring himself to shoot Duff, and didn't like to think of Tate doing it, either. "I won't," he said. "I hain't like you or Tate. I can't shoot and kill a help-less man in cold blood."

A grim smile cut across Duff's face. He opened his eyes and glared at Hamp. "Cold blood? Nawsir! Mine's exactly same as yours, even if you buchra don't want to believe it."

"Well, you seem to think us *buchra* is all alike," Hamp

shot back. "Can't trust a one of us, hain't them your words?" He shook his head. Trying to talk was useless, a waste of time. He strode over to fetch Bone.

Duff turned his head away when Hamp bent to lift Bone up, but he grabbed Hamp's wrist. "Here's the truth of it, for all it's worth," he said, his voice hitching. "Damn Yanks killed Massa Gavin. They shot him. I dragged him off to the side of the field, trying to save him. Was me that hid us both behind a tree, thinking we could stay there till the litter corps come to carry off the hurt and bury the dead. Me that stroked his head like I'm his nanny. We stayed there seemed like hours but must've been only one, listening to the devil's work and praying to God.

"The patch of red on that fine coat Mistus sewed for Massa Gavin bloomed wide as a camellia flower, then a dinner plate, then it stained the whole front. Massa Gavin crying all the while, like he did when we was young'uns. Spitting up blood, and saying he got hisself killed for nothing. 'They should've give you a gun,' he said, over and over."

Duff rocked forward for a second and held his face in his hands. He made fists against his eyes and pressed them in hard. "I shushed him and pulled the coat open to look. Find he's got a hole in the gut. Powerful stink from it put in mind chitlins during hog butchering, and I emptied my stomach on the ground right there. Both of us know being gut-shot means you die slow, and hurt terrible bad. Even so, I told him, 'You'll be fine. Lie still.'"

Duff stopped again. His shoulders shook. When he

Kim L. Siegelson

spoke again, his voice sounded small and forced. "Gavin tells me he's cold and so thirsty, then he start talking out of his head. Like he's somebody else, somebody crazy. He shoves his gun at me and says to help him. I thought he meant shoot Yanks for him, but he draws it around toward his face. 'No, I ain't doing that,' I say, and try to pull it away, afraid it'll go off accidental. But he holds on with all his strength, all that's left, and yells at me, 'You my darkie, boy! You do what I tell you! You do it! Shoot! Shoot!'

"He ain't never talked to me like that, so angry and mean," Duff said, his voice wavering and hoarse. "Never been like his daddy, or his brother. Never hurt me. I knew he meant it. I knew. So I . . . I done what he asked."

Hamp felt as wrung out and thin as the half light that filtered through the cloudy sky. There were no words to say. No way to answer. Nothing right.

Duff tipped his head up. His face was twisted with misery. "But I didn't do it because I'm his boy, his slave he can boss. No! I saw his suffering! How can a man see suffering and do nothing? God send my soul to hell for what I done, I don't care no more." He covered his face with his hands again and held them there, weeping in great heaves.

Watching him, Hamp was afeared. Not *of* Duff, but for him. "I got to go," he said. "I'll come back, and I'll bring someone. Take care of Bone." He turned to leave, then stopped. Without speaking, he knelt and reloaded the musket, laid it and the shot bag on the ground where Duff could reach them. Then he turned and ran toward the water.

Pellets of rain pattered the surface of the swamp until it looked like hammered copper. Hamp dug into it with the old paddle and felt the dugout jerk forward. It was a long, heavy boat and didn't glide the way a punt did. But it held him and Julius and Ruth and Mercy. Julius stroked with the broken paddle, but he didn't know the rhythm of it and his chopping turned them in circles, so he stopped and let Hamp do it alone.

But for the dip and splash of the paddle, and Ruth humming to Mercy, they traveled in silence. They'd been easy to find on Bugaboo. Too easy. Even a poor tracker like Scrub could've found them by the smoke of their fire, built beneath an open-side shelter of thatched branches. Lucky he'd got to them first. And if luck held, Scrub and Tate were miles west, still searching the thicks around Billy's Island, moving toward the outlands.

He told Ruth and Julius nothing but that they'd be found if they didn't go with him, and he'd take them farther south where there was another runaway who needed help. They hadn't argued or doubted him. In the time it took to snuff their fire, they'd packed their few things to go. Together, he and Julius tore the shelter apart and scattered it, and Ruth brushed the dirt clean of footprints with a gallberry branch.

Hamp hoped that Duff and Bone were where he'd left

them, and that Duff hadn't tried to run, hurt as he was. It had taken a full day to reach Bugaboo, but less on the return south with a light wind at their backs.

By the time they reached the edge of the island, it'd stopped raining, but the sky looked low enough to rake a hat from your head. Felt like late afternoon, though it was hard to gauge with the light slanted askew so by cloud, and tinted blue. He skirted around the shore until he found the right channel inside and then the narrower strand that spurred from it. Before the boat touched land, he dropped his paddle and jumped into the water and pulled it. His pants billowed around his legs like water-weeds.

"I don't know how bad he's hurt, but we need to get there before this freshet comes up into a downpour," he said.

He helped Ruth from the dugout, then she took Mercy from Julius and they followed him to the clearing, leaving their trumpery behind. The sodden embers of his and Duff's dead fire stared upward from the center of the camp like the fixed, unblinking eye of the island. But for the gunnysack, and Duff's hat, and the dead boar, it was empty. But for the crackle of twigs beneath their feet and the whistling birdcalls, it was quiet.

The wind left him. Bone and Duff were gone.

Ruth sucked her breath in at the sight of the huge hog, and Mercy clung tighter to her shoulder. To Hamp the boar smelled more terrible than when he'd left. A gaggy rancidness hung in the air despite the drizzling rain.

Buzzards and jackdaws sat in the treetops, surveying the bounty. Eventually, the other rooters would return to feast. Julius looked at it with awe and shook his head. "That thing's a half or more bigger than me. Watch for snakes and gators, you said. I don't recall you warning about this."

A thin, sad moan issued from the boar and Ruth scurried back from it. "Lord, it's living yet," she whispered. "Like something out of the devil's own mind."

"It seemed killed when I left," Hamp said. "Look at the blood on the ground under it. Nothing could spill so much and live."

He picked up a stick and edged toward the boar, careful of each footstep, watchful that it didn't scramble to its feet. The jackdaws cawed in alarm as he drew near. Then he saw that the boar's eyes looked sticky and blank. Flies clotted at their corners. The smell overpowered him and he retched. When he jabbed the hog with the stick, it didn't stir, but another moan and then a yelp escaped from it. Sounded like a dog. No other than Bone.

He found them jammed behind the bulk of the boar, almost beneath it. Duff had both arms wrapped around Bone and one hand clamped to his muzzle. The two of them were caked with blood and dirt. The stench was powerful.

Hamp held his arm over his nose and breathed through his mouth.

"I didn't know where else to go," Duff said. "Hurt to breathe or move." He took a couple of short, gasping breaths and held his left arm tight against his ribs. His knee had swollen to the size of a small melon. "You didn't say who you's bringing. I figured it might be Tate."

"No. Bone wouldn't like if I did. Mightn't come home with me."

"He's a good old dog," Duff said. He loosened his hold so Hamp could take Bone. Then Julius lifted Duff and laid him beside the fire ash.

Ruth sent Julius to fetch their trumpery from the dugout and a tin of water, while Hamp set about rekindling the fire and making shelter. She tore her underskirt into long strips to bind Duff's ribs and his knee.

"When the water warms, I'll clean the blood off," she told him. "Then I'll bind you tight enough it'll help ease the pain, so we can travel. We hear you're heading south to Florida to find your sister. We'll take you if you'd let us, as payment of a favor we owe to someone." She cut her eyes toward Hamp, but he knew she meant Neeta.

"You know the way?" Duff asked.

She shook her head, then gestured to Hamp. "He'll point us the right way, and we'll get there by and by. We'll make it."

Hamp nodded agreement. "I believe you will."

Julius returned with the water, and Duff gripped the tree trunk while Ruth worked on him. Bone leaned against his leg and licked his hand until she'd finished. Then Ruth inspected the gash on his flank and said, "Let me fix you, too, hound."

Thunder rumbled and rolled above them and the first

scattered drops of rain rattled through the trees. *God's thunder, not man's,* Hamp told himself. God's seemed gentle in comparison.

He and Julius finished thatching the rough shelter with dry palmetto fronds. They stowed Mercy inside while Ruth twined the last strip of cloth around Bone's hip and leg.

Hamp squinted up into the falling droplets. Closed his eyes and let them splash over his face and shoulders and arms. It felt clean and cold.

The rain rolled off Duff's shoulders and arms, making streaks through the boar blood. He gestured at the snug lean-to and asked, "Ain't you coming inside?"

Hamp shook his head. "No. I want to get closer to home. I been gone a long time, somebody is bound to come looking for me. I'll point them away from here."

Neither of them made move to part, and Hamp asked, "You think everything'll be different after the war?"

Duff shrugged one shoulder. "I hope at least one thing'll be different."

"Amen," Ruth murmured.

Hamp flinched. "But the South will have to lose for that to happen. What about soldiers like my pap, who didn't go warring over slaves? Them that fought for love of their home, them that died for it. All they want is freedom. It hain't fair."

Julius put his arm over Ruth's shoulders and wiped the other across his brow. "Ain't this our home much as it is anybody's? Born here same as any Reb fighting, and we

Kim L. Siegelson

want nothing but to live here and be free, same as them. Can't if the South wins this war. That ain't fair, and it ain't right."

"No matter who wins, folks won't just drop their hard feelings and get along," Hamp shot back. "We're split too wide now."

More than Yanks and Rebs, or black and white, he was thinking of him and Pap.

"You got to start somewhere, even if it takes a hundred years to finish," Duff said, "even if you die trying. It's the only good that can come of it."

They fell quiet. Hamp listened to the soft rattle of leaves shedding water and wondered if Pap would agree with Julius, and if he would understand about Duff. Seemed too long since they'd talked. There was so much to talk about besides the swamp. Everything else in the world.

"Take some of that boar meat and dry it in strips over the smoke before you go," he told Julius. "Shouldn't go to waste, and you'll need it."

Julius held his hand out and Hamp took it this time. It felt strong and warm and rough, just like Pap's.

"I'll tell Sumi about you when I find her, swamper," Duff said.

Hamp slipped his hand in his pocket and fingered the bird whistle, then drew it out and held it toward Duff. "I shouldn't have took this."

Duff reached for it, but rather than take it, he folded it inside Hamp's hand. "Keep it," he said. "I'll make her another. And I'll remember the birds that go with my feathers, and tell her a swamper name of Hamp knew how to talk to them and call them from the trees."

He leaned forward and whispered so only Hamp could hear. "The bird on the tip end of that whistle is a jay. They have feathers blue as heaven, edged with black. Jay is the name I chose for myself . . . Just so you'll know."

He petted Bone one more time. "I'm gon' get me a dog just like this 'un down in Florida. Spoil him rotten, too."

Hamp grinned and pushed the whistle deep into his pocket. "Hain't another one like this 'un, nowhere." He lifted Bone and slung him across his shoulders, and put Pap's gun across his back, then ran from the clearing without looking behind. Without saying good-bye. He'd take the dugout and follow dark, winding water across the swamp and all the way back to Duck Pond Lake. Leave Ruth, Julius, Mercy, and Jay to find another way, along a different path.

Someday, after the war, maybe their paths would cross again.

Head bowed against the drizzling rain, Hamp dug the paddle into Duck Pond. The blue light had deepened into early dark, and the rain had come and gone in fits. He pulled the boat ashore on Duff's Island and unloaded the little inside it, and turned it over so the rounded bottom shed water. He'd hide it there, rather than take it to Rooter Island. There'd be fewer questions if anyone found it. Both he and Bone were shivering and numb from the drizzle, and a powerful hunger had come over him. He slogged across the shallow lake, keeping close to the shore, and took the well-worn path to the camp on Rooter Island as quick as he could. The thought of spending the night there so cold and empty stripped him raw, but he'd not set up a shelter before leaving, and the firewood would be too wet to take a flame.

Exhausted, he stumbled over every root and dip in the path, and finally put Bone down to limp along on his own. They moved slow as old turtles, hunched against the weather. Then Bone stopped of a sudden, lifted his head and yodel-called.

Another dog answered him, and in a blink Rascal rushed on top of them from the shadows. Bone twisted and wriggled and whimpered and beat his tail while

Rascal sniffed him from nose to tail, scenting the boar still on him.

"That you, Hamp?" It was Pap's voice calling.

"Yessir!" Hamp answered. Dread made him feel colder still, rooted in place. He gathered himself and took a deep breath and stumbled toward the platform. Pap had set up a lean-to of canvas soaked in beeswax to keep off the rain. He wobbled as he stood, and the two of them took each other in through the softening, gray veil of rain. It ran off Pap's hat brim in uneven streamers that spattered around his one bare foot.

Hamp felt a rush of thankfulness. Pap had come looking for him. He wanted to run to him and tell him everything. But he didn't. He held back and waited for Pap to speak first.

Lightning pulsed through the dark and made Pap's face look pale beneath his hat brim, and his eyes were hidden in the shadow that it cast. The skin over his hollow cheeks was drawn tight as a tick. He seemed to be searching for words, something to say. The corners of his mouth trembled, and Hamp felt the familiar heat rise inside him.

Pap bent his head so that all Hamp could see was his hat crown. "Your ma was worried."

"She needn't be," Hamp answered, his voice sounding harsher than he'd wanted. He dropped his head, too, and pinched a drip of rain from the end of his nose.

Pap wavered slightly, or maybe the wind pushed him. He took two steps toward Hamp. "I told her you could take care of yourself. You didn't need me out tracking behind you. You've learned all you care to from me, and know all there is in the world to know." He sounded bitter, full of disappointment.

Hamp flinched and swallowed the sting in his throat. What he wanted to say was, *I know more than you think, Pap, but I need you anyway.*

Thunder rolled in the distance and Pap jumped at the noise. He took off his hat, wiped his face with his arm and looked out over the swamp as the storm moved away toward the east. Bone limped and Rascal trotted over to him, and they rested their rumps nearly on top of his toes. Bone pushed his knobbly head beneath Pap's hand and sagged against his leg. Hamp wished he was Bone, that he could push himself next to Pap like that. But the space under Pap's hand seemed too small for him now.

"That freshet ought to do a lot to help fill up Okefenokee's creeks again," Pap said. He looked strained and skittery as a fawn.

Duff had said thunder made him think of cannons and battlefields. Maybe it'd be a long time before thunder just sounded like ordinary thunder to Pap. God's thunder.

"It'll fill, along and along," Hamp agreed, gently. "Some things takes time and can't be rushed. Hain't that what you always told me?"

The corners of Pap's mouth turned up a stitch. "You remember that?"

"Clear as I remember that gobbler call you taught me." Hamp put his hands to his mouth and sounded it. "Yessir,

I remember most everything you ever said. But I had to figure some things on my own, while you was gone. Didn't have no choice."

This time Pap flinched. "That hain't easy for me to swallow sometimes, Hamp. I can still picture the day you was born and your ma and me named you." His jaw twitched as he stared off into the trees.

Hamp brushed his fingertips over the outside of his pocket and felt the hard lines and angles of the carved whistle. "Almost thirteen years since you called my name the first time. Gre-gre-granpap's name, too, a true born swamper with swamp water for blood—like me and you."

Pap set his hat back on his head. A smile flitted over his face quick as a waterbug across a puddle. He took a deep, slow breath and held it like he didn't want to let it out. Finally he did. "Been a long time since we sat out here and talked, hain't it? Them was good times, easier days."

"Still could be," Hamp said. "And we can talk on Pinder just as good as we can out here, can't we?"

"Yep," Pap answered, nodding. "I have to say Neeta hain't never been short of talk or secrets." He turned and gave Hamp a sidelong look that said he knew everything.

It was like he'd figured. Neeta couldn't keep a secret. "You won't tell Scrub, will you?" he asked.

Pap shook his head. "Maybe you don't think my going off to war was the right thing to do, same as I don't understand why you and Neeta done what you did. But I know your ma and me raised you to know right when you see it. To stand your ground without buckling under." He leaned against his crutch and bobbed his head. "I'll trust in you that much, if you do the same for me."

For a moment Hamp felt like he'd caught a glimpse of someone out of the corner of his eye, someone he'd been looking for. He joined Pap and the dogs inside the canvas shelter. They sat together without talking, listening to the thunder fade into soft rumble that finally melted into the gentle night music of the swamp. They watched the dark for a while and then slept, and woke when first light crept in to soften the sky toward mornglowm. Seemed like God had opened his door a crack to check on things.

The peeper frogs trilled with voices bigger than their thumb-sized bodies. A jaybird swooped overhead, and landed on a sunny limb in the gumball tree. It gowered at Bone and Rascal before it settled back, fluffing its blue feathers to dry them. A gator bellowed from his wallow somewhere close by. Back at Pinder Island the resurrection fern would have begun to unfurl into green fronds all along the rain-soaked tree limbs. They'd look feathered by now, like they might up and fly off into the blue.

"We best get going or your ma and Neeta will worry about the both of us and send Scrub," Pap said. He fumbled for his crutch. Hamp leapt to his feet first and held out his hand for Pap to take. He braced himself as Pap pulled up, balanced his weight until they stood facing each other, eye to eye. Steady.

Beneath them the thinnest of roots trailed down from the island's underbelly through dark water, searching for a place to latch on to, a way to shake hands and never let go. Any swamper could tell you that roots and time enough could build something solid and steady the trembling earth.

BIBLIOGRAPHY

Fisk, Carol, writer/producer. *Swampwise [With Okefenokee Joe]*, a video recording. Georgia Public Television, 1990.

Harper, Francis, and Delma E. Presley. *Okefinokee Album*. Athens: University of Georgia Press, 1981.

Mays, Lois Barefoot. *Settlers of the Okefenokee: Seven Biographical Sketches*. Folkston, GA: Okefenokee Press, 1975.

Neimeyer, Lucian, and George W. Folkerts. *Okefenokee*. Jackson: University Press of Mississippi, 2002.

Ransom, Candice F. *Children of the Civil War*. Minneapolis: Carolrhoda Books, 1998.

Rappaport, Doreen. *Escape from Slavery: Five Journeys to Freedom*. New York: HarperCollins, 1991.